Grave Instinct

Bev Pettersen

Published by Bev Pettersen, 2020.

Copyright 2020 Bev Pettersen

Westerhall Books

Editor: Pat Thomas

Print ISBN: 978-1-987835-21-2

To R.K.'s wonderful Main Street neighbors and small town saviors.

PROLOGUE

NIKKI DRAKE PULLED in a cautious breath and crept closer to the hay bales, relieved they let her remain unseen. Stacked five feet high, the bales were a full inch taller than her head. She rose on her toes, craning over the hay toward the sound of laughter. Just as she feared, her sister Erin posed at the end of the aisle with the wealthy boarders, acting like she didn't have a care in the world...or a long row of stalls to clean. She'd pushed her wheelbarrow behind a saddle rack as if hoping everyone would forget she was a lowly stable hand.

Voices bubbled as the girls spoke about their afternoon trail ride and how today's route would take them beyond the brook and through a stand of California oaks. Erin would be delighted to be included and Nikki was relieved to hear her laugh. But it meant she'd have to clean her sister's stalls again today.

She sagged against the hay, tired and confused. A year ago Erin had been obsessed with horses. Cleaning stalls at the local stable in exchange for riding lessons had been their dream jobs. But it seemed her sister had flipped a switch when she hit fifteen. Now all she cared about was clothes, makeup and complaining with the older girls—the ones rich enough to own their own horses, who always had their noses tilted up and dressed as if they were riding in the Olympics.

Those girls weren't even real friends. Friends wouldn't whisper behind Erin's back or make fun of people shoveling manure. But there wasn't much Nikki could do. She needed Erin to *want* to come to the barn. Their mother wouldn't drive twenty miles after work to pick up only one daughter. It was always double or nothing. And Erin was the oldest, the one who dictated their after-school activities.

Nikki adored her sister but deciphering her frame of mind was bewildering. And Erin needed constant attention, not just from their mother but from outsiders. Otherwise she moaned and sulked and descended into dark moods, and there was that time she thought she was fat and wouldn't eat, not even when Nikki made Erin her favorite desserts.

However, their mother was worried and that only fanned Nikki's determination to help. She'd do anything to make her sister smile, to get her best friend back, but it seemed Erin had changed when she started wearing makeup. It sucked that Nikki wouldn't have time for her riding lesson today, something she'd worked all week to earn, but at least a trail ride would leave Erin in a good mood. And cleaning extra stalls meant Nikki would have a reason to be around the big jumpers.

Those horses were so majestic that simply leading them to their paddocks was an honor, even if they pulled too hard on their lead lines and sometimes hurt her hand. Besides, if she worked quickly cleaning the stalls she might finish up in time to practice braiding. Plaiting manes was an excellent way to make money. On show days, the boarders paid a fortune to anyone who could properly braid their horses' manes and tails.

Time would be tight though. The shavings pile was on the other side of the barn, and the huge box stalls would each need three and a half wheelbarrows of shavings. Filling them with fresh bedding took almost as much time as mucking out the manure.

Squaring her shoulders, she hurried back down the aisle. Erin was responsible for cleaning six stalls. Five of the stalls were empty—the horses were turned out in paddocks for the day—but the sixth stall contained a towering bay mare. Despite her size, the mare needed a separate turnout or else she was picked on by the others. Even Stormy, the smallest pony in the stable, chased her around unmercifully, something that the other kids found amusing but Nikki thought was mostly sad. Nothing bothered her as much as a bully.

"Give them a swift kick," she said, clipping on a lead line and eyeing the bay mare's massive feet. "Bet then they'd leave you alone."

"I bet they would too." Justin Decker's amused voice sounded behind her. "But size doesn't equate to toughness. Just look at you and Stormy."

Nikki gave a wary smile at her boss who was standing by the stall door. She'd had a little fight on her first day—not a fight, more of a dust-up really—but Justin never forgot how she'd stood up to one of the biggest boys. She used to be intimidated by Justin. He was a great instructor and could ride the wildest animals, even Diesel, who pinned his ears and shook the ground whenever he bucked.

At first she'd thought Justin was one of the privileged boarders but later learned he was working his way through university and had been around horses all his life. The stable owners trusted him completely and rarely visited the barn when he was around.

His half smile turned to a frown. "What are you doing with that mare?"

"Turning her out so I can clean the stall." Nikki's words came out a bit defensive but she wanted to prove she could handle the big jumpers almost as well as Erin. Sure, maybe the big horses dragged her around a bit but she'd never once let go of the lead rope, no matter how far they pulled her. And she didn't need anyone looking out for her.

"But this is Erin's section," he said. "And your hands are already rope burned." She gave a silent groan. Justin noticed everything. He'd already turned toward the sound of giggling, his eyes narrowed. Three of the four girls were boarders—they paid to keep their horses here. They could laugh and laze around all they wanted. But Erin wasn't a paying customer. She was supposed to be working.

"I promised Erin I'd clean her stalls today," Nikki said quickly. "And my hands are much better today so I can work really fast."

Justin didn't like animals standing in dirty stalls longer than necessary and always worried about the horses. He'd fired a girl for feeding an hour late, although one rumor said the real reason was because she'd shown up wearing a swim suit top.

Nikki made a mental note to keep an eye on Erin's clothes. Lately her sister had been changing at school and wearing her riding clothes on the bus. It was weird to wear an expensive pair of breeches to shovel manure, but Erin seemed to be copying the rich girls, from their hair and makeup right down to their clothing.

But what if the boarders started wearing skimpy tops? Justin couldn't kick out the boarders but he was in charge of barn help. And he was a stickler for rules. He was still frowning, looking back and forth from Nikki's hands to the cluster of girls at the far end of the barn.

"They're going on a trail ride," Nikki explained, giving a vague wave down the aisle. "So I *want* to clean Erin's stalls. And just skip my riding lesson with you."

Justin tilted his head and for a moment she thought everything would be okay. Then his mouth firmed. "I already set up the pony jumps," he said. "Besides, these stalls aren't your responsibility. This is the third time this week you've had to clean your sister's stalls. I'll have another talk with her."

Nikki's fingers tightened around the lead rope. Justin was already turning away, his tight shoulders showing it wouldn't be a friendly chat. But Erin would be mortified if he chewed her out in front of the boarders. Doubly mortified because Erin had a ridiculous crush on Justin. All the older girls did.

"Wait," Nikki called. "Don't say anything. Don't, please...Justin." She stumbled over his name, hated asking for favors. Besides, pleading wouldn't help. Justin was like a bossy older brother, and not the type to change his mind.

But surprisingly he turned, folded both arms over the top of the stall door and waited. Everyone said he could make both people and animals listen, simply by leveling his intimidating stare. He rarely used that look on her. Had always been patient, even at the beginning when she didn't even know how to properly halter a horse.

His dark eyes pinned her now though, as if he could read every thought, and that wasn't at all comfortable. She stilled, just like one of the horses he handled so effortlessly. Silence stretched and she began wiggling. Then the truth came out.

"It's just that Erin feels better if everyone likes her." Nikki's words escaped in a rush. "This is the first time those girls ever invited her on a trail ride. It's important to her so I want her to be able to go."

Something flickered in Justin's expression. He no longer looked so bossy, only resigned. "I can't let this continue. You've been doing the bulk of her work. There are others who would love to have her job, kids like you who work and listen and appreciate the chance to be here. Besides, lately she's been impatient with the horses."

Nikki swallowed the growing lump in her throat. Everything he said was true. She hated how Erin misused her spurs when Justin wasn't around. But she couldn't imagine how empty her own life would be without horses. There wouldn't be a single bright spot left.

"Erin has to stay." Her voice cracked. "Or I won't be able to work here either."

The mare edged sideways, picking up on Nikki's distress, almost squashing her toes with a plate-sized hoof.

Justin yanked open the stall door. "This isn't a teen hangout. And don't let that mare push you around. Make her listen or else you could get hurt."

Naturally the horse turned stock still as soon as Justin entered the stall. Usually Nikki brushed off any help, but today she let him pry the lead line from her hand. He never let a horse get away with bad behavior. People either. And it had been a mistake admitting the truth. Justin was her boss, not a friend. She should have said Erin had a headache or a sore arm, even a painful menstrual period. Anything would have been better.

"You're too small to safely handle these jumpers." Justin continued to scold, his voice as disapproving as her school principal's. "That's why I assigned you the pony section. And you can't do your work properly if you keep blistering your hands."

Her shoulders slumped and she stared at the toes of her boots, guessing he was going to send her packing along with Erin. But his next words surprised her.

"Now tell me why you can't be here without your sister," he said. "You come on the bus, correct? Is it the drive home? Maybe I can find someone who's going your way."

She jerked her head up, astonished by his offer. They both knew that if Justin asked, any number of parents would volunteer to drive her home. But the good feeling vanished as quickly as it had come. Her mother didn't trust Erin to be alone. And if Justin fired Erin, she'd need cheering up; she'd need Nikki's company. That's the way it always worked.

"Don't worry," Justin said, studying her face. "I'll figure out the driving. But you need to accept that Erin no longer shares the same interests. It's no big deal. It happens a lot with the older kids."

"She likes to ride though," Nikki said, crossing her arms. "She's really excited about the trail ride. And if she can ride with those girls, it will change everything."

Justin shook his head. "Trail rides take too long. And remember the rule: No working, no riding."

"But couldn't you let me do her stalls again, just for this week? Because I know my sister. Once she feels good about herself, she'll be back to normal and then she'll be even better at her job." Nikki crossed her fingers, not completely certain Erin would ever be content mucking out stalls. But desperation left her scrambling.

Besides, it didn't matter what she said. Judging by the set of Justin's jaw, it was clear he wouldn't change his mind. She'd seen that look before and it never boded well for the person on the other end. She pressed her hands over her stomach, physically sick at the thought of not being able to see her favorite pony. Knowing Stormy was waiting to greet her, ready to trot out and receive his apple, helped her make it though the boring school day.

"I can't make exceptions," Justin said. "It's not fair to all the other kids who work so hard. But don't worry. There's no reason you can't keep your job. I'll make sure you have a way home even if I have to drive you myself."

His kindness only made her gut roil again and she hated the way her eyes itched. But she felt helpless and embarrassingly close to crying. She certainly wasn't going to admit the truth, that her older sister was acting weird and couldn't be left alone or—and Nikki had learned to accept it as fact—that her mother loved Erin more than her.

She settled her quivering breath and raised her head, knowing she couldn't leave here without a fight. "If you let me work out the stalls with Erin," she said boldly, "I'll wash and groom your horses before every show."

She didn't want to think of how much time that would take or how she'd ever fit in any more riding lessons. But at least she and Erin would still be able to come to the barn.

Justin's expression didn't change, but she sensed his surprise. She definitely had his attention. He didn't even notice the mare was sniffing at his pocket, a familiarity he didn't usually permit.

"I'll braid their manes and tails too," she added, guessing that offer wouldn't have much value. Justin could braid a horse in his sleep: tight beautiful plaits while hers were big and loose, and usually fell out as soon as the horse started to trot.

But he just looked at her with those dark eyes. Then he gave a little nod. "All right, Nik. But you need to put the horses in crossties and use the mounting block, not the tippy stool. And wear gloves the rest of the week. There are some extra pairs beside my tack box."

"Really? We have a deal?" Nikki gaped for a moment then solemnly stuck out her hand, not caring about her blisters, scarcely daring to breathe until he shook it.

But this was so incredible it was hard not to jump in delight. Justin's word was like gold. He always did what he promised and he could never be coerced. Even when a boarder's father had demanded Nikki cool out his daughter's fancy show pony, Justin had refused, saying it would be better if the pony moved to another stable. And when he was teaching, he never wasted time by talking to adults, no matter how expensive a car they drove.

Two hours later, she was still bouncing. No one ever negotiated with Justin but she'd done it. She and Erin had a reprieve.

Her sister had looked so happy heading out on the trail with the older girls. Of course, the three boarders had been mounted on their long-striding hunters and Erin had been on Pancho, her placid lesson horse. But her sister had worn a beautiful smile beneath her new helmet, delighted just to be included.

"I can't believe I have the rest of the afternoon off," Erin had whispered. "This is perfect, thanks to you!" She'd even twisted in the saddle, giving Nikki a grateful wave before disappearing in the trees.

But now the air had chilled and the day was dissolving into dusk. Nikki peered out the doorway, rubbing her arms and scanning the trail. She'd finished dumping shavings in the stalls much faster than expected and even had time to braid two manes. But now she was eager to hear about the ride. The girls should be back soon. None of the riders wore jackets and their horses would be eager for their evening grain.

At least Erin would be in a good mood after the trail ride. Crossing the brook was always fun. Justin had taken Nikki and Erin out there many times, and brook jumping was high on their list of favorite things.

Finally voices sounded in the distance, followed by the drumming of hooves. Three horses trotted out from the towering trees, with riders perched high on their backs, girls with fancy black helmets and perfect white smiles. They were talking about low-hanging branches, jumping the brook, and how hard it was to trot and get a really good selfie.

Nikki scooted from the barn. "Where's Erin?" she asked, peering past them into the gathering gloom.

The first rider, Kimberley, looked blank then glanced around the open doorway. "Isn't she back yet? We haven't seen her since she didn't want to jump the brook."

"What do you mean?" Nikki jogged alongside the sweaty horses, staring up at the riders, stung by a prick of alarm.

"She couldn't keep up," Theresa, the second rider said. "So we told her she should go back to the barn. It was the best thing."

The best thing? Nikki jerked to a stop, then turned and stared down the dark trail. Erin would be devastated. Pancho too.

She swung around, her fists clenching. "It's never the best thing. No horse likes to be ridden alone in the woods. Even a quiet horse like Pancho. And if you don't know that by now, you're all idiots."

She wanted to call them worse, but unlike Justin, her sister didn't appreciate it when Nikki stood up to the older kids. Now though, it would be doubly hard to build up Erin's confidence. Hopefully by the time she returned, Nikki would be able to convince her that these selfish girls weren't worth anything but pity.

She even started rehearsing, knowing from experience what her sister would like to hear: that Theresa had a frog face, that Kimberley had been caught cheating on a math test, and—Nikki's ace in the hole—that Justin said Erin was a better rider than all three of them.

She paced back and forth outside the barn, thinking about what she'd say and how to say it. But she never had the chance to pump up her sister. Never had the chance to help her unsaddle Pancho or reassure her about how much nicer she was than those three entitled girls. The pep talk didn't happen.

Because Erin never came back.

CHAPTER ONE

T *welve years later*

NIKKI DRAKE PROPPED her feet on her office desk and leaned further back in her chair. It wasn't the most professional of poses but she didn't have many drop-in visitors and never this early in the morning. Clients had to drum up their courage before hiring a private investigator, especially when it involved cheating spouses. Adultery cases were her least favorite but she had to take them to pay the rent. And to keep Gunner in premium dog food.

She reached down, trailing her hand over her Shepherd's head. Gunner lay on his mat close to the base of her swivel chair, a position where he could watch both her and the door. Judging by the prick of his ears someone had entered the stairwell. Odds were good that the person would stop at the office closer to the steps. Sonja's Psychic and Parties received more visitors than Nikki's fledgling investigative company.

Sighing, she continued scanning her email, warming at the message from a recent client. Thank-you notes were rare but always motivating.

"You deserve the credit on that one, Gunner," she murmured. The lady's wandering Shetland pony had squeezed beneath a fence and fallen into a deserted well. If not for Gunner's keen nose, no one would have checked the overgrown brush that concealed the deadly hole. Not in time anyway.

Not all her cases were that simple or ended so happily. Most of them were boring, especially the snooze-inducing surveillance that came with her job. Robert Fletcher, family friend and the man who had mentored her in the business, had taught her to concentrate on insurance fraud and infidelity. That way she'd be assured a regular paycheck. But her true passion was reuniting families.

Unfortunately she never landed that type of case. And now that Robert had retired, she had to bring in her own business. But five years' experience, three of them as a lowly apprentice, didn't instill confidence from potential clients. Families of the missing wanted proven track records. She'd felt the same way back when her sister disappeared.

Gunner's tail thumped, announcing a visitor and one he welcomed. She knew it was Robert by his familiar tread and the sound of humming. But breaking news at the bottom of the screen grabbed her attention. For a moment she quit breathing. A teenage girl hadn't returned from a trail ride. And just like Erin, the horse had been found. But not the rider.

The door clicked open. She glanced up, staring mutely at the silver-haired man who'd entered her office. He balanced two cups of coffee along with a paper-wrapped dog bone in his left hand before deftly closing the door behind him.

Her gaze jerked back to the news bulletin, her breath escaping in a horrified whoosh. "I have to go! A teenage girl is missing. And it sounds like the same barn where Erin disappeared."

"I heard." Robert set the coffee down and settled into the visitor's chair. "That's why I dropped by so early. Because you need to sit back and not tear off like some vigilante."

"But I need to get out there." She unlocked her gun drawer, almost bumping Gunner who was sitting now, nose twitching.

"Let's discuss this first," Robert said, his voice as calm and reasonable as when he'd taught her to swim. "You know the police won't let you near the scene. Are you sure it's the same riding stable?"

"It has to be. They don't identify it but there's only one big horse barn on Quarry Road." She laid her Glock on the desk and peered back at her screen, hungry for details. "Maybe this person took them both. That could mean Erin is still alive."

"It's been twelve years," Robert said. "The probability—"

"I know." She paused to reassure Gunner who stared up at her, alarmed by the firmness of her voice. But she didn't want Robert to finish the sentence, even though she accepted Erin was likely dead. The details around her sister's disappearance were just too murky.

Erin's horse had been found by the brook, tied to a tree bordering the clearing. The lead line had been safely attached to the halter beneath Pancho's bridle. The knot had been a proper quick release. A horseperson would never tie a horse by the bridle reins, but the average abductor wouldn't know that. The stirrups had also been raised so they wouldn't get caught on a tree or thump Pancho's sides.

Accordingly, police had concluded Erin dismounted, made sure her horse was safe then walked out of the woods on her own. So they probably hadn't searched the area as thoroughly as they should have. Nikki's belief there'd been a less-than-proper search still nagged at her.

The disappearance of a second girl changed everything. Maybe a predator was holding the girls in an underground bunker. That area was a perfect place to hide. The woods were so thick that both riders and hikers stuck to the trails, with the brook serving as a natural boundary.

Or maybe there hadn't been an abduction. Maybe there was an abandoned well, just like the one that had trapped the Shetland pony. Searchers had concentrated on the wooded area between the stable and the clearing where they'd found Pancho, but maybe Erin had walked in the opposite direction, too hurt and embarrassed to return to the barn after being dumped by her pseudo friends. She *could* have fallen into a concealed pit.

Nikki gripped the sides of her desk, tortured by thoughts of Erin dying—slow and alone—at the bottom of an overgrown hole. Her sister had always hated to be alone. She reminded herself that Erin's phone had never been found, and Erin wouldn't have hesitated to call Nikki. Maybe not the first half hour but she wouldn't have left Pancho tied to a tree any longer than that.

She would have asked Nikki to walk to the clearing and collect him...unless her phone was smashed. Falling into a hole could have done that, which would explain why the police had never been able to trace it.

Nikki pried her fingers off the desk, her thoughts crystallizing. Robert's advice was always sound and she knew it was prudent to slow down and process this development. In her most optimistic scenarios, her sister was living on a Caribbean island, in the arms of a wonderful man who had whisked her away from mean girls, mucking out manure, and a stubborn little sister who'd just wanted Erin to keep liking horses.

But with this new rider missing, it seemed more likely that Erin had been abducted. And Nikki didn't have to process any more. She certainly wasn't going to sit back and wait. Because if that predator were still out there, she intended to find him.

Robert was busy removing the wrap from the dog bone, and she didn't want to waste time arguing. He'd been the best man at her parents' wedding and was always supportive, more like a father figure than anyone else. Once Robert realized she'd never give up looking for Erin, he had mentored Nikki in his office, insisting she put in the hours and earn a proper investigative license.

He'd even sent her to Japan to strengthen her aikido training and though he'd retired his license three years ago, he was always available for a consult. He was one of the few men Gunner trusted, although any dog would adore someone who kept a supply of meaty bones on hand. She didn't always follow Robert's advice, but she always gave him the respect he deserved.

Tamping down her impatience, she watched as Gunner lifted the bone from Robert's outstretched hand. He lay down on his mat, the bone between his paws and then stared up at her, asking for permission.

"Okay," she said, waving a hand. She'd let him enjoy the bone for a few minutes because Robert was correct about one thing. The police would never let her near the scene. Robert had worked for the force for twenty years before becoming an investigator. He knew how they operated. As a result, so did she.

"How would you handle this?" she asked, ostensibly putting away her Glock and picking up a pen.

"Wait," Robert said. "See what the police turn up. The girl's name is Savannah Whynot. If she remains missing, the family will be more open to hiring their own investigator. I have a friend who's checking into their finances. Remember, you can't afford to take any more cases without pay."

She doodled on a sheet of paper, pressing the pen much harder than necessary. They both knew she had her own views about compensation and further discussion would only waste time. She hadn't entered this profession to become rich. Her goal was to help, and she especially wanted to help families like hers, ones who couldn't afford an investigator. She'd been paid well for finding the pony so she had enough in her bank account to cover this month's expenses. She certainly had enough gas to drive out to Quarry Road. The area adjoining the west side of the property was state-owned and too big for the police to block access. And nothing was going to stop her from searching for this girl.

"I'll check with my contacts," Robert said. "Hopefully they'll find her before the day is out. But if they don't, and it turns out to be the same stable..." He gave a slow head shake. "This could be our breakthrough. We just have to be patient."

She nodded, trying not to glance at the computer as he went on to speak about the perils of working personal cases. She'd heard his warnings so many times, knew firsthand how hard it was to remain objective. Admittedly, patience wasn't her strong suit, especially when Erin might still be out there.

"So you see," Robert added, "it's easy to miss critical details when you have such a personal stake. Best to let the searchers do their job. When I get back, I'll make some calls. Find out what they know and we can work from there. In the meantime, I had an inquiry from someone who wants security for a silver anniversary party. Sounds like the perfect gig for you. I asked him to forward all the details."

He rose and nodded goodbye, murmuring about an early tee time. In the far corner, Gunner gnawed on his bone, his tail thumping contentedly as Robert strode from the office.

"Leave it." Nikki shot from the chair the instant Robert's steps faded. Tossing her pen aside, she scooped up her gun and backpack. Robert was methodical and experienced and she valued his advice, but he was much too plodding. There was no way she was going to sit back and twiddle her thumbs. Not when this new disappearance might be related to Erin.

Besides, she might be able to help find Savannah. She didn't have a trained police dog by her side when her sister disappeared. Now she did.

CHAPTER TWO

"HERE'S A COFFEE FOR you," Nikki said, as she stepped into the adjacent office, although office was hardly the proper word for the exotic space Sonja had created. Even Gunner seemed intimidated by the crystals, candles and hint of incense.

"And that is why you are my most favorite person in the world," Sonja said, gratefully accepting the cup and waving at a cushioned wicker chair. "Do you have time to sit? My next client cancelled."

"Can't." Nikki shook her head. "Heading out on a job. Don't even have time to drink the coffee Robert brought."

"I assume this job is something in the woods." Sonja's nose wrinkled as her eyes swept over Nikki's T-shirt and tight ponytail. "You'd have more men than Robert in your life if you ditched the jeans and hairy dog."

Nikki grinned. At first she'd been wary of Sonja. They had completely opposite tastes in clothes, politics and pizza. And Sonja's impassioned talk about energy and free will was always disconcerting. However, the woman's flamboyant style hid an insightful intelligence and love of animals that Nikki appreciated.

"It's hard to work in a skirt and heels," Nikki said.

"Not if you're doing insurance jobs. I thought you were going to focus on clients who actually paid their bills. I don't want you losing your office space."

"That won't happen." Nikki spoke firmly, shutting down the subject.

Sonja pursed her lips but said no more. And despite her joke about Gunner, she was already reaching into a glittering crystal bowl, something she kept filled with treats ever since "the hairy dog" had protected her from an abusive visitor. Reality was Sonja had plenty of hairy critters of her own. She even looked after Gunner on her hobby farm when Nikki had out-of-town jobs and a couple times had dressed him up as a lion for her psychic parties. Though neither woman fully understood each other's profession—nor wanted to—they had developed a genuine friendship.

Sometimes Sonja's flare for clothes reminded Nikki of Erin. Maybe that's why Nikki had let Sonja break down her customary reserve. Robert, however, remained less than enthused that a psychic had moved into the adjacent office.

"It makes your PI business look unprofessional," he'd said. "Sonja's just another self-proclaimed expert. I don't believe in all that hokey pokey stuff."

Neither did Nikki. Although only six months ago she'd thought she spotted Erin working the streets and was so convinced she'd agreed to have a psychic reading. Sonja had squashed her fear that Erin had been forced into prostitution, but made it infinitely worse when she'd stated Erin was dead and that Nikki wouldn't be happy until she let go of her self-blame.

That had put a chill in their relationship that had lasted weeks. Now Nikki politely declined any offers of psychic services, even something as simple as a tarot reading. She valued their friendship too much.

"Can't you sit down for five minutes?" Sonja pleaded. "Surely your client can wait that long."

"It's not a client," Nikki said, keeping a firm hand on the door handle. "It's personal. See you tomorrow."

Gunner looked similarly disappointed that they weren't staying but Sonja tossed him a dog treat. He caught it in the air, devouring it in a crunching bite as he followed Nikki out the door.

They circled around the building to the back alley where Nikki usually jammed her car. Already the smell of freshly baked pizza filled the morning air, mingling with shampoo and soap from the adjacent barber shop. The tattoo parlor was still locked, but the owner of the consignment shop gave Nikki a cheery wave. This was a blue collar area, occupied by a motley range of businesses. Robert had suggested she take over his office in a more established part of the city but the rent had been astronomical, and she didn't want to owe him anything more than she already did. Besides, this area and the people suited her. It also had a spot filled with grass and hardy dandelions that was excellent for dog breaks.

Gunner jumped into the back of her Subaru and forty minutes later, they'd escaped the city traffic and turned onto the pitted blacktop toward Quarry Road. She slowed, peering through the windshield for familiar landmarks. This area was a mix of farm and woodland, never densely populated, and the bumps that had rocked the school bus had deepened.

She veered around a jagged pothole that would have shredded her tire then checked on Gunner who was sprawled behind her on the fold-down seat. His head rested on his paws, but his eyes and ears were alert, studying the grazing animals with interest.

He seemed equally at home in the country as the city. While Sonja kept a variety of rescue animals on her farm, Gunner hadn't been exposed to horses much, at least to Nikki's knowledge. She'd stopped riding the day Erin disappeared.

Those first years had been rough. Her mother had withdrawn into a shell, alternating between stony silence and accusations, followed by weepy apologies. Nikki's guilt had twisted into anger. She'd spent more time fighting in school than learning. Robert had done all he could, dropping off groceries, paying for therapists and trying to help them manage their grief. However, he hadn't been able to help her mother.

Nikki's fingers tightened around the wheel and she glanced back at Gunner again, comforted by his solid presence. He was staring at something to his right, and she followed his gaze, surprised she'd almost driven past the stable.

The barn looked smaller, the white rail fences not as tall or impressive. It was definitely the search hub though. Trucks, trailers and all-terrain vehicles clogged the parking lot. From this distance it was impossible to see if there was a K-9 unit on site. Media vans were parked on the shoulder of the road but a deputy blocked the driveway with his car. The whole thing was sickeningly familiar and her gut clenched with foreboding.

She forced her sweaty hands to loosen and continued past the gravel driveway. The deputy scowled, probably labeling her as rubber-necking sightseer. Obviously she wouldn't be allowed entry. But the presence of empty all-terrain trailers confirmed the search was still active. One positive, at least.

Besides, she didn't need to use the front entrance. A network of public trails crisscrossed the land adjacent to the stable, and she'd ridden on many of them. It would be impossible for police to block every trailhead.

She passed four pickups manned by solemn volunteers in yellow bibs who motioned for her to continue driving. They were obviously positioned to keep trails clear from contamination in case this turned into a crime scene. They'd done the same thing when Erin had disappeared, although it hadn't helped. The theory that Erin had tied Pancho, then walked out to the road and left in a vehicle had never been substantiated. There'd been too many tire tracks and the ground had been too dry to provide any supporting evidence.

Nikki drove another pensive mile, weighed down with thoughts, theories and dark memories. The blacktop changed to gravel, the road empty now of vehicles. But there used to be a narrow bridge where the brook cut Quarry Road and marked the perimeter of public land. If she could find the brook, she could gain access.

She slowed, scanning both sides of the road, searching for the bridge and the game trail that used to follow the east side of the brook. The path had been too narrow for big horses but a plucky pony like Stormy had no problem fitting between the trees. She'd ridden the trail often, delighting that she could go where no one else could follow, pretending she was a pioneer in the wilderness, just her and a rather cantankerous pony.

Thinking of Stormy made her smile. He'd been so naughty, few children wanted to ride him, but at one time he'd been her best friend. She was so wrapped up in her memories she would have missed the bridge if not for the crunch of gravel over planked wood and the changing vibration of her tires.

Sobering, she jammed her vehicle onto the narrow shoulder and yanked open the back door.

"Let's go, Gunner," she said, grabbing her backpack and clipping on his leash.

They scrambled into the overgrown ditch, ducked beneath a rotting tree and then were instantly slowed by a prickly wall of brush. Twice she had to stop and untangle Gunner's leash and she began doubting her memory.

Was this the wrong spot? There didn't seem to be any sort of path. However, the brook couldn't have changed and the game trail had followed it to the road. She remembered her mother picking them up by the bridge when they owed money for Erin's riding gloves. It had been a week before payday and her mom hadn't wanted to drive by the owner's house.

So Nikki pushed on, punching through an endless stretch of bramble that grabbed at her clothes and pricked her skin.

Finally she found it—a narrow mossy path that snaked alongside the brook. The spot where Erin's horse had been found was still miles away but that was only if one stayed on a groomed bridle path. As a crow flew, or a little pony walked, the clearing was much closer.

She didn't like to think about that clearing. Or what might have happened there. But it seemed history was repeating itself, and she was determined to help. Maybe a predator who knew girls rode alone in these woods had built an underground lair. Perhaps he'd taken Erin but after more than a decade was bored, wanted a replacement and had grabbed Savannah.

So Nikki inched forward, checking bushes, tree roots, old stumps, searching for a ventilation hole, the depression of a trap door, vegetation beaten down in an odd way, anything that would reveal a hidden human presence. It took ten minutes to travel thirty feet and when Gunner gave her hip a questioning nudge, she realized she was letting emotion cloud her focus.

This was about Savannah. It was just as likely the unfortunate girl had fallen off her horse and needed medical attention. Nothing related to Erin or secret bunkers or scum who preyed on solitary women.

But she couldn't stop her shiver. Because this was definitely the perfect place to stash a victim. Few people would willingly push through these claustrophobic bushes, not without good reason. She certainly couldn't imagine any normal person choosing to hike here.

Gunner stiffened, his head raised, his ears marking a sound only he heard. Moments later, she heard something too.

"Quiet," she whispered, dropping to her knees and placing a warning hand over his muzzle.

Gunner's attention was locked on a rustling less than a stone's throw away. A rabbit or mouse? Perhaps another searcher? But legitimate searchers wouldn't be in this area and they'd be moving in a grid, calling Savannah's name. These sounds were subtle, like someone who preferred not to be seen and was accustomed to moving silently.

Keeping her eyes glued toward the sound, she slipped the pack off her shoulders and reached inside, searching by touch. Rubber ball, pepper spray, gun. She pulled out her Glock, comforted by its familiar weight, hoping it was *him*. For years, she'd yearned to punish the man who had taken her sister.

But this was a prime spot for an ambush, his advantage, and her heart thumped with adrenaline and fear. The surrounding brush was so thick he could be on her in an instant. She couldn't unleash Gunner. Not yet. Her dog could move much faster than her and she didn't want him facing danger alone. Fortunately she could depend on his keen nose to tell her the direction of the man's approach, and she'd rather have Gunner beside her than anyone else. Her dog was loyal, smart and ever suspicious.

An ant crawled across her hand and overhead a blue jay screamed. But she kept her attention locked on Gunner, relying on his instincts. He would never be fooled by someone posing as a hiker, and all she needed to do was follow his lead. But her eyes widened at his odd reaction. Gunner wasn't growling. His lip hadn't curled. Even his hackles didn't rise.

Only his tail moved. And it was wagging.

CHAPTER THREE

NIKKI GAPED IN DISMAY. Gunner was always suspicious of men and this was a bad time to turn friendly. But he was wiggling with such delight, he resembled an overgrown Lab pup rather than a reserved police dog. Then realization struck. She'd thought she'd evaded the police by coming in by the old bridge, but there would be no fooling this particular cop.

A branch moved and Justin Decker stepped out. He'd filled out over the years, and he seemed even taller today, especially since she was kneeling on the ground. No sense trying to bluff, pretending she was just out walking her dog. Not with Justin. He knew her too well.

"Hello, Detective," she said, quickly slipping her gun back in her pack.

"You shouldn't be here, Nikki."

His greetings were often terse but at least he wasn't calling his officers to escort her back to her car. He, of all people, would understand why it had been impossible for her to stay away. Erin's disappearance had impacted his career choice as surely as it had her own. But policing suited him. He'd risen quickly in the ranks, from beat cop to top detective. And though it was probably prudent to make up an excuse, she'd never been able to lie to him.

"I wanted to help," she said, rising to her feet, ignoring the dirt that clung to her jeans. "And I didn't cross any police lines. I didn't think anyone knew about this trail."

"Your pony trail?" The left side of his mouth twitched, making him look much more approachable. "I knew."

She tilted her head, remembering the time someone had chopped up a fallen tree too big for Stormy to jump. She'd never known who had walked all the way out with an axe, only that she'd been grateful her secret trail was no longer blocked. And if Justin knew about this path, he would have known about its accessibility by the bridge.

"Do you know if this area was thoroughly searched?" she asked. "Back *then*."

His mouth flattened and he looked at Gunner, his way of letting her know he was in charge of the questions. He had an effective deadpan and his dark sunglasses made it hard to read his expression. Of course, Justin was always difficult to read.

"Gunner looks good," he said. "Still using the same commands?"

"Most of them." She glanced down at Gunner who lay obediently on the ground. The only thing not still was his tail. It has been Justin who had brought her Gunner when the dog turned two. He'd flunked out of police training so had been free to a good home.

"What did he fail?" she had asked.

"Ladder climbing or something," Justin had said. She'd been dubious about dog ownership—both the attachment and the responsibility—but as usual, Justin had been right. She'd fallen in love with Gunner, and his training had helped her in countless situations. And that was probably her best card to play before Justin sent her packing.

"I thought Gunner could help look for Savannah," she said, hiding behind a confident tone. "He found a pony last week and he's had a lot of practice tracking animals on my friend's farm."

"He always had a good nose," Justin said. "No one ever argued that." He keyed his shoulder mic, his thoughtful gaze on her dog as he spoke to someone called Tony.

At least she hadn't been banished. And he was letting her listen to his conversation with the command post. Obviously Savannah hadn't been found yet. Based on his questions, a chopper was in the air, equipped with a heat sensor. A K-9 team was working the horse trails but it sounded like that dog was miles away and moving in a northwest direction.

Justin clicked off the radio, his eyes sweeping her pack. "I assume you have Gunner's tracking harness in there. Put it on and let's see what he can do. I'll have someone meet us at the clearing with a piece of Savannah's clothing."

Nikki gave a grateful nod. However, she'd been hoping for a general search, one where Gunner might alert them to a possible predator. But if Gunner was told to find Savannah he'd likely ignore any other scent, even if they walked over an underground bunker.

"This area is so isolated," she said, reaching into her pack. "It's probably best to have Gunner search now. I really think that would be best."

"Best for whom?" Justin said. "This isn't about your sister. Savannah is the one we need to find. There's a better chance she's alive."

His blunt words left her fumbling with the harness. She'd accepted the police had moved on. Robert and Sonja also believed Erin was dead. But hearing a similar thought from Justin twisted something deep in her chest. She bent over Gunner, hiding her vulnerability, hating the way her fingers trembled. The snap was too stiff or too small, and she couldn't force the damn thing over the metal ring.

Justin reached out, his arm pressing against her thigh, his warm hand covering her fingers. He didn't say a word, didn't even clip the snap. He was just there. Emotion swamped her: anger, frustration and something else she felt whenever he was close, a sharp level of attraction that she kept buried.

"Today has to be about Savannah," Justin said. "But I'm still looking for Erin. Like you, I'll never stop."

Her breath came out in a grateful whoosh. Everyone thought Erin was dead. The police rarely returned her calls now and when they did, it was with a hint of impatience. She'd thought becoming a licensed investigator would give her an inside edge. But there had been no suspects, no witnesses, no evidence. Even Robert had given up. To have Justin still solidly on her side made her feel much less alone.

He understood her pain and guilt. Privately she might admit her sister was never coming back. However, it wouldn't be the cold hard truth until they found a body. And deep down she craved justice. She needed to see Erin's abductor punished.

Her throat thickened and it was tempting to turn and tuck her head against Justin's chest. To close her eyes and curl up in a ball and let him comfort her, as he had that horrible day when Erin hadn't returned.

"But you have to think of another missing girl now," Justin went on. "Gunner won't be able to do his job if he senses you're upset. And I'll be wasting my time with you, valuable time that Savannah can't afford."

Nikki jerked back, horrified to think she was wasting precious seconds. Justin always knew how to motivate her. And she appreciated his dose of realism. Her sister was a cold case while Savannah might be able to go home to a warm bed. She wanted to make that happen. So badly. Perhaps in the process she'd see something that would uncover the mystery of what had happened to Erin.

Squaring her shoulders, she tightened her grip on the tracking rope, aware Gunner would pick up every nuance of her voice and body. "We're ready," she said firmly. "Let's go find Savannah."

CHAPTER FOUR

THE BRUSH WAS THICK and dense and while Gunner was able to push through, Nikki and Justin were forced to move much slower. The long lead kept tangling, consuming more precious time. And Gunner still hadn't picked up the scent.

When she'd first shown him Savannah's shirt, Gunner had stuck his quivering nose in the cotton and bounded off, delighted to have a job. But now his enthusiasm waned and he kept glancing back, his eyes a question. Judging by his behavior, it didn't appear that Savannah had been anywhere in this section of the woods. But Nikki tamped down her negative thoughts. This was Justin's show, and she was grateful he was letting her help.

"Hold up," Justin said, his voice as even as if he was sitting behind a desk. "Take a break and I'll radio in our coordinates."

Nikki nodded, relieved to give Gunner a break even though it was obvious Justin didn't need one. However scent dogs could easily hyperventilate since their noses were working overtime. She pulled out a bottle and a collapsible bowl then sat beside Gunner while he noisily lapped the water. Heat and perspiration glued her shirt to her skin. It felt as if they'd covered a lot of ground but progress was frustratingly slow.

It was easier to pick up a scent if Gunner could run in an open field and spiral out from the center as he did at Sonja's farm. Sometimes he detected it in the air rather than following a trail.

But if Savannah was being held underground—and Nikki couldn't push the bunker idea completely from her head—it was unlikely Gunner would pick up the girl's scent unless he was very close.

She twisted the cap back on her water bottle, trying to keep thoughts of Erin from bleeding into this search. But as usual, it was impossible to stop thinking of her sister.

Justin was still talking on the radio, his voice deep and composed, even though he must be similarly frustrated. She could hear the conversation and it wasn't reassuring. The helicopter hadn't spotted any sign and the K-9 team had turned up nothing. Just like Erin twelve years ago, Savannah had vanished into thin air.

Justin clicked off the radio. "How's Gunner feeling?"

It was typical of him to worry about animals, but in this case even more practical. A tired or hurting dog might ignore a scent.

"He's good," she said. "With a break every twenty minutes or so, he can continue."

"What about you? Feeling okay?"

"I'm great." She wasn't tired, but the backs of her heels were rubbing and soggy socks meant blisters were inevitable. She should have detoured home and grabbed her waterproof boots. However, she'd been in too much of a hurry. She'd never imagined she'd be allowed to join the official search. Had anticipated scoping the area beside the brook or, at the very most, to be checking the game trail outside the perimeter. And for this unexpected opportunity, it was no problem blocking inconsequential pain. All she had to do was think of Savannah's family and the agony they were enduring.

She started to rise but Justin placed a hand on her shoulder. "Stay down," he said. "Rest for another minute. Want something for your blisters?"

She peered up and caught the amused twitch of his lip. "How did you know?"

He tossed her some band-aids then crouched down and pulled a bramble from her pony tail. It should have hurt, but his fingers handled her hair as deftly as when he used to plait a horse's mane. She tilted her head, giving him better access, accepting she didn't always have to act tough, at least with him.

"That feels nice," she said, blowing out a pleasurable sigh.

He instantly dropped his hand. "I just don't want you slowing down Gunner."

They both knew brambles and blisters wouldn't slow her down. But lately Justin didn't seem to want to touch her. He'd already moved away, putting more distance between them. And Gunner had his head on his paws, watching them both with concern. He lived to please, knew that if he was successful she'd pull his red ball from the backpack and they'd have a fun play. So far though, he hadn't been able to pick up any scent to run a track. Of course, Savannah had been mounted for all or most of the time.

"Where did they find Savannah's horse?" Nikki asked as she ripped open the band-aids and stuck them on her heels. "Is it possible she fell off over one of the cross-country jumps on the north side?"

"Her horse galloped back to the barn so we don't know where he came from. And those old hurdles are gone. The stable is full of endurance riders now."

Nikki grimaced. Now she understood why the searchers seemed to have no idea of Savannah's route. With a big horse, typical of the jumpers, the rider would stick to groomed trails where it wasn't necessary to duck beneath branches. But the endurance riders sought out more challenging terrain; their horses were smaller and more nimble. A good horse could travel a considerable distance in four hours, unrestricted by obstacles such as water, thickets and steep hills. Hopefully Savannah hadn't been on a good endurance horse.

"Savannah's horse was an Arabian, 14.2 hands high and very fit." Justin spoke as if reading her mind. "When she rode out yesterday, she was headed toward the brook. Her cell phone was found in her bag, attached to her saddle."

Nikki grimly tightened her boot laces, praying that Savannah had fallen off and not been abducted. Justin had always insisted riders carry their phones on their person so that if they fell off, the phone didn't disappear with their horse.

When Erin had vanished, police tried to trace her cell but it appeared as if the chip had been removed. That was another bothersome detail. Erin never would have dismantled her cherished phone, even if she knew how to do it. But in Savannah's case, it made sense she hadn't called for help—her horse had carried the phone back to the barn.

"Maybe the dogs should be tracking the horse, not the person," Nikki said.

"One team already tried that. But there's too much scent. The barn wasn't closed for riding until late last night and the K-9 kept getting sidetracked. He couldn't discriminate between the horses."

"Gunner might lock onto the Arabian though. He spends a lot of time at Sonja's farm tracking her goats and llamas. We make a game of it and he always finds the right animal."

Justin scrubbed a skeptical hand over his jaw. "That's asking a lot. Especially since Savannah's horse is standing in his stall. His scent will override all his older trails."

"But what if they brought us the horse's saddle pad?" Nikki scrambled to her feet, galvanized with fresh hope. Even Gunner whined, affected by her energy. "We'll stay far away from the barn," she said. "I bet he can pick up the scent from the back end. At least enough so we can narrow down the search area."

Justin looked at her, then at Gunner. He must have seen the confidence in their expressions because he gave a little nod. "Okay," he said, reaching for his radio. "It's worth a shot."

CHAPTER FIVE

NIKKI WAITED AT THE edge of the clearing, too far from the officials to pick up much of the conversation. Justin was doing most of the talking. Occasionally a word or two drifted her way as they discussed GPS markers on a deployment screen. This area was the hub for the searchers, although she didn't see any other scent dogs.

Gunner sat close to her hip, alert but untroubled by the air of urgency. His composure was reassuring. If he'd acted too aggressively, she doubted Justin would let him participate. She took him so many places, in such a variety of situations that Gunner wasn't aware he'd soon be occupying center stage.

It was her own composure she was battling. This was the same clearing where Erin's friends had deserted her, where Pancho had been found tied to a tree. The area had been a favorite spot for riders because it had fresh water, green grass and even a couple apple trees. A deep-banked brook bubbled in the background, three feet wide at its narrowest spot. A quarter mile downstream was a sandy approach where more cautious horses and riders could wade across. But not here. In this spot, the only way to cross the brook was to jump.

Erin had stood in this same clearing, alone and abandoned. But why had she dismounted? Had Pancho acted up when the other horses left? Had she been afraid to ride him back to the barn? Or simply too proud? Those questions plagued Nikki. If only Erin had texted her. Justin would have given her permission to take Stormy out to join Pancho. He always worried about safety, emphasizing that horses were herd animals and therefore calmer with others.

She remembered his concern when she told him that Erin and Pancho hadn't returned, and that she wanted permission to ride out to find her. It had taken about ten minutes to locate him and she'd still been incensed at the boarders. No doubt, Justin had regretted letting Erin leave her chores and go on the trail ride. But he hadn't snapped or complained. He just studied Nikki for a moment, as if assessing her anger.

"Stay here, kid, and calm down," he'd said. "I'll be faster on Diesel." He hadn't wasted any time tacking up. Instead, he'd grabbed a rope and halter, swung up on the horse's back and galloped off. Even then, she hadn't been too worried. She'd been angry at the girls and felt bad for Erin, but at that moment she'd mostly been impressed at how well Justin could ride bareback.

Gunner shoved his nose in her hand, his worried eyes on her face. He had no idea why she hated this clearing and the stable, or that they were the reason for her recurring nightmares. But he always picked up on her turmoil. She gave him a reassuring pat, aware she had to stay focused. There was a lost girl out here, frightened and possibly hurt, who needed to be found.

One thing for certain, Savannah hadn't followed the secret game trail to the road. Gunner had cleared that section. And a K-9 unit had checked the other trail heads. Which meant Savannah must still be somewhere in the woods.

Nikki caught Justin's authoritative head jab and a tall plainclothes officer detached himself from the group. The man walked up, stopping a respectful distance from Gunner. The bulge beneath his shirt proved a handgun was tucked in his waistband.

"I'm Tony Lambert, the K-9 coordinator." He gestured at a red all-terrain vehicle. "Help yourself to sandwiches and coffee, and there's plenty of water if you need to replenish. That's a big Shepherd," he added, his gaze lingering on Gunner. "Don't see his type much in SAR. He looks like the ones we have on the riot squad."

Tony seemed to think she was with search and rescue. It was probably wise not to announce she was a private investigator. Some police resented PIs. "Gunner might come from the same breeder," she said "He had some police training before he flunked out."

"Oh, hell. Is that Gunner? I remember him. He wasn't as quick as the Malinois but he was capable. And he didn't flunk out, not exactly. He just refused to climb. He also was getting aggressive. We planned to send him to the protection unit until Justin bought him."

"Bought him?"

"Yes. When Gunner was about a year and a half. Paid a chunk of money too."

Nikki coiled the dog lead, hiding her confusion. Justin said Gunner had failed some critical tests and that's why he was free to a good home. She never would have adopted him if he hadn't needed to be rescued. And she didn't get him until he was two so Justin must have had Gunner for at least six months. That explained why the dog adored him.

It was obvious Gunner didn't have a similar affection for Tony. He wasn't growling or straining at the lead, but his eyes were locked on the man's throat and his raised hackles made him look even bigger. Not surprising. Gunner was always suspicious when a man showed her any attention. It helped with her job but it was hell on boyfriends, especially if they didn't understand dogs.

Tony, though, was clearly a dog man. He remained chatty and relaxed, hands at his side, talking about the K-9 training facility and the differences between air scenters and ground trailers. And as she relaxed, so did Gunner.

"You should drop by our open house in November. See the facility where Gunner had his formative training." Tony gave a little wink. "And the ladders he couldn't climb to save his life."

"I'd like that," Nikki said, totally grateful her dog had a weakness that resulted in him leaving the force. Gunner had turned into her best friend when she hadn't even known she needed one.

"There's also jerky in the cooler," Tony said, gesturing at the four-wheeler again. "I can bring it over if you want to keep Gunner away from the odors. And don't worry about carrying water for him. Searchers will be behind you with supplies. Do you want to lighten your load?"

"No, thanks. I'm good." She adjusted the strap of her backpack. It barely weighed eight pounds and she always ran with it, maintaining her strength and endurance. Of course, there was no anticipating where Gunner's nose would take them. Certainly it would be much rougher terrain than her daily jogs. But she preferred to be self-sufficient. Had learned not to rely on anyone.

She just hoped Gunner would lock onto Savannah's Arabian and not be confused by the other horses. He was usually successful playing the "find" game at Sonja's farm and it was one of the ways she kept him in shape, physically and mentally. Hopefully that training would make a difference.

"Do you have the Arabian's saddle pad?" she asked.

"Sure do." Tony gave a wry nod. "It reeks of sweat and we also rubbed it over the horse for the last twenty minutes. Not sure if it will be enough though. Our other K-9s were confused with all the scents."

It was cool how Tony included Gunner with the scent dogs and Nikki felt a rush of confidence. She rocked on her toes, impatient to get started. But it was important to control her adrenaline and keep her breathing level. It would be disastrous to burn out the first five minutes and turn into a dead weight at the end of Gunner's lead.

Tony nodded in understanding. "I'll leave you two alone to get ready then," he said, and her impression of him rose a notch.

She walked Gunner in a circle, keeping their muscles loose and visualizing their job. The first few minutes would be a sprint. Once she showed Gunner the horse's saddle pad, he'd be off like a bullet, nose down, searching for the scent. She'd be sprinting too, gripping the twenty-foot line, trying not to slow him down or curb his enthusiasm. She wouldn't let him loose, not in this unknown terrain. Gunner became so focused on following a scent he could hurt himself on briars, rocks or barbed wire.

The burning question was if he'd realize it was a specific horse he was tracking or if he'd be distracted by fresher scent. Nine other riders had been here yesterday, searching for Savannah after her horse galloped back to the barn, riderless. Hoof prints crisscrossed the ground, joining a network of riding trails that fanned from the clearing. And that wasn't even considering the trails on the other side of the brook.

She knelt beside Gunner, wrapped her hands around his head and stared into his soulful eyes. "You're a good dog!" she said, pumping him up. "Ready for the farm game!"

Justin had given her a handwritten notebook on Gunner's care as well as the dog's commands. Some of the more lethal ones were in German, and "farm game" certainly hadn't been on the list. But those were the words she used when searching for animals on Sonja's farm and they had worked brilliantly when he'd found the pony stuck in the well. She'd also learned that if she kept things light Gunner focused better, worrying less about pleasing her and concentrating more on the find game.

Although in this situation, it wasn't a game. Tracking this particular horse could save Savannah's life.

CHAPTER SIX

NIKKI OPENED THE PLASTIC bag and held the Arabian's saddle pad in front of Gunner, letting him get a good whiff. White hair clung to the bottom of the pad but it wasn't as sweaty as she'd anticipated. That didn't seem to matter though. Gunner sniffed it eagerly, his nose twitching.

Behind her, Justin and his group waited. Silent and hopeful.

"Find!" Nikki said, dropping the saddle pad. Someone following her would pick it up but she needed to move quickly. Already Gunner had shot out, almost yanking her off her feet. He zigzagged across the clearing, nose to the ground. She raced behind him, the lead double twisted around her right hand. Gunner's ears were pricked, his body taut as he charged forward, darting to the left, to the right and then shooting forward again.

Twice he headed down riding trails cut with hoof prints but both times he wheeled and returned to the clearing. He appeared to be looking for an individual scent, seemed to know the difference between Savannah's Arabian and the rest of the horses. However Nikki's hope was short-lived as he swung toward the red four-wheeler and scrambled up on the seat. He sniffed at the cushioned seat, then sat, wagging his tail and looking very proud.

Her heart sank. *Was he distracted by the food?*

Tony ran up, his expression sheepish. "Savannah's horse brushes are beneath the seat," he murmured. "Sorry."

"Find," she said, keeping her attention on her dog.

Gunner gave a happy yip, leaped off the machine and powered toward the brook, delighted the game wasn't over. But he was heading in the wrong direction. The barn owners had already told them the Arabian didn't like to jump the brook, that Savannah always used the sandy ford further downstream.

But Gunner pulled on the lead, tugging her forward. She followed, steeling herself for waist-high chilly water. But he didn't power across the brook. Instead, he wheeled to the left, squeezing past a briar bush and down a narrow game trail that headed away from the water.

Certainly a big horse couldn't fit along the trail, but other than the brambles at the beginning it wasn't impassable. Not for a small Arabian. However this route was a dead end. She remembered the trail maps and knew it led to the back of a limestone quarry, long ago abandoned. There was nothing left but a deep pit surrounded by spiked rocks and invasive trees.

She scanned the ground as she ran, looking for hoof prints, anything that would give her confidence to trust her dog...and almost tripped over Gunner who'd jerked to a stop close to a water-filled brackish pit. She stared in dismay. They'd barely traveled a quarter mile and had clearly wasted the searchers' time. Savannah wouldn't have ridden to the quarry. No rider would.

But Gunner sat beside a stunted tree, wagging his tail, signaling his find. And he didn't usually make mistakes.

She studied the tree, her attention caught by a skeletal white swathe. Bark had been rubbed off at the exact height one would tie a horse. To the right of the tree, hoof prints cut the ground, leading to a wider path that headed east. Back to the barn.

"Good dog," she said, scanning the obvious horse trail.

Gunner shot forward, taking her words as a signal to continue. She quickly checked him. There was no sense letting him trail the prints back to the barn. They already knew Savannah's horse was back in his stall; it was where the gelding had been that was important.

This didn't make sense but it certainly appeared Savannah had been here. Judging by the amount of manure, her horse had been tied to this tree, long and often. Flies crawled over one of the mounds, indicating it was fresher than the others. And white hairs fluttered in the breeze where the horse had rubbed his mane against the bark.

"Good dog!" Nikki repeated, patting Gunner's head and pulling the red ball from her backpack. She tossed him the ball, all the while talking in the singsong voice that he adored, letting him know his job was done.

Gunner didn't share her triumph. He squeezed the ball between his strong jaws but looked rather puzzled that she hadn't let him find the live horse. She crouched beside him, reassuring him that he was a good dog. The best.

But she still couldn't understand what he had found. This place was too close to the stable. Who would saddle up and ride to this bleak spot, heavy with the smell of stagnant water, only to tie their horse to a tree? There was barely any grass and the water certainly wasn't drinkable, for horse or rider.

Justin jogged up, not even breathing hard from the run. His eyes swept the site then he raised a hand, motioning for the searchers to stay back.

"Put these on," he said, passing Nikki a pair of plastic booties. He barked orders into his radio and a woman in a ball cap began calling Savannah's name.

Justin hadn't moved since passing her the booties. Now he knelt beside her, staring at the ground, at the tree then at the brackish water. The ball squeaked between Gunner's jaws. Flies buzzed and a squirrel scolded. But Nikki didn't speak, understanding Justin's need for silence.

"Why would a sixteen-year-old girl pretend she's going on long trail rides?" he finally said.

"Maybe her parents were pushing her to ride," Nikki said. "Maybe they thought horses would keep her busy and out of trouble."

Justin ran a hand over his jaw. The stubble had darkened over the last hours, making him look more like a criminal than a detective. "Didn't sound as if they were worried about that," he said. "Not from the interview. In fact, the parents said she was a horse nut and didn't date. Her only male friend was the boy next door."

Nikki refrained from making the obvious comment. That boy would have been the first to be questioned and Justin didn't appreciate needless chatter. Probably the reason he had liked her as a stable hand was because she hadn't talked and giggled as much as some of the other girls.

"Gunner came through for us." Justin's gaze angled over the ground as if he were reading a book. "He definitely followed the right horse. Savannah's Arabian wore bar shoes in the front but was barefoot in the back, just like what we're seeing. It looks like she sat on a blanket by the tree."

Nikki followed his gaze, trying to read the sign. She knew the difference between a shod and unshod hoof, but the bar shoe and blanket had escaped her. She hadn't even noticed the rectangular impression, clearly a blanket now that Justin had pointed it out. A blue thread even gleamed in the sun.

She felt a stab of disappointment. Part of her had been hoping to find a hidden shack and that Erin would step out, alive after all this time. But a blanket proved Savannah had chosen to sit there. She hadn't been abducted.

Gunner dropped the ball and licked her hand, then reached out and did the same to Justin, as if determined to be fair. He tilted his head, his eyes concerned, obviously still worried that he hadn't found a live horse.

"I'm going to let him follow the tracks back to the barn," Nikki said. "So he can find the horse and finish the job."

"No. Don't move. Not even an inch. Technicians are on their way."

The steel in Justin's voice made her freeze. Then he did something even more strange. He grabbed her hand.

"What's wrong?" she asked.

"I wish you didn't have to be here," he said. "I never wanted you to see this."

She stared in bewilderment. His voice was gentle yet deep with remorse. His shoulders were as tight as his grip, and if her dog didn't know Justin so well, he probably would have grabbed Justin's arm.

A flash of yellow caught her eye. Justin's team was already stringing up crime scene tape. She'd heard him on the radio barking out orders but hadn't absorbed all his instructions, too busy praising her dog and hoping Savannah was close by.

Justin wasn't looking at the officers. His eyes remained locked on her face. She'd never seen him look so apologetic. And sad. He was stroking her hand now, and his intimate touch would have been welcomed if she weren't so confused. "I'm going to need an impression of your boots," he said. "As of now, we're the only two searchers who have walked here."

She'd assumed Savannah was hurt and lying somewhere close by. But he was treating this as a crime scene. "What are you seeing?" she asked.

"Missing rocks. Flattened weeds. The drag marks."

She peered over their joined hands, staring in dismay toward the water. Something definitely had been moved. And in three spots the ground was pitted with holes as if rocks had recently been moved. There was even a partial boot tread, much too large for a teenage girl.

"Divers are on the way," Justin said. "But I'll get you out of here before that."

"I'm a PI," she said. "I've seen dead bodies before." Mostly pictures though. And Justin knew her usual clientele. Knew she'd never been hired to work a missing-person case. Or a homicide.

Bile climbed her throat. She swallowed, trying to block her thoughts. To stay objective. But the images unfolded in her mind: a sexual tryst, a fight, then a helpless girl weighed down by rocks and dumped in that ugly green water. Had Savannah been alive when she went under? And despite her resolve to hide her horror, Nikki flinched.

"I shouldn't have let you come," Justin said, his voice gruff. "But I needed you and Gunner."

"At least her family will know," Nikki muttered.

Justin leaned closer, squeezing her shoulders but still managing to hold her hand. He had kept her at arm's length for so long, it was rather unexpected. She could feel the pounding of his heart, as if he were equally disturbed. And he'd been exposed to so many brutal homicides his emotion now was rather surprising.

Realization hit.

"You think Erin's in there too?" she said, surprised her voice was so level.

"It's a possibility," Justin said. He wasn't looking anywhere but at her face. Not at his waiting officers or the drag marks or at that ominous water. He was really worried. Seemed the only thing he ever felt for her was concern. She didn't want that. Besides, he should be thinking of finding a murderer, possibly even the man who'd taken Erin.

She pushed his hand away. "I'm fine. Do what you have to do. Gunner and I will stay very still and not contaminate the scene any more than we already have."

Justin's expression changed, his face turning to a hard mask. "I'll have someone pick you up as soon as possible," he said. "You'll need to leave the same way we came in."

With that, he unfolded from the ground, leaving empty air where his arm had been.

CHAPTER SEVEN

THE SUN WARMED NIKKI'S shoulders, the sky an optimistic blue, but the quarry held a tomblike quiet. Even the scolding squirrel had hushed. Gunner nosed the ball closer to Nikki's knee, oblivious to the splashes of the recovery team in the water only twenty feet away.

She tightened her grip around his lead. Gunner didn't understand why she wouldn't throw the ball. Now he thought he hadn't done his job when he most certainly had, and incredibly well. But it seemed sacrilege to be tossing a ball in the air while police divers were in that cloudy water, searching for a body. And Savannah's family was waiting, afraid yet still hopeful. If Justin's instincts were correct, that hope would soon be dashed.

Maybe it was better to have a body. To know, rather than to forever wonder. Still, a sliver of hope must be better than no hope at all. She knew she didn't want Erin's body to be found tucked beneath that bank, despite the closure it would bring. And she fervently prayed Savannah wasn't in there either. That trail of crushed grass didn't have to mean a person was dragged. It could be something else. Oh God, she prayed it was something else.

At the moment, two people in coveralls stood on the bank, one with a long stick and the other holding a rope. Divers had gone in less than five minutes earlier. Justin remained on the side of the bank, standing beside Tony, two technicians, and another detective. They looked grim, not talking much, their eyes unflinching.

She focused on the water spiders skimming over the surface, reminding herself that this was a valuable learning experience. And it was important to copy the mannerisms of these professionals who did their jobs, no matter how gut wrenching. So she squared her shoulders and tried to look all steely eyed.

But the side of her mouth wobbled because it was impossible not to think of Erin. To imagine what might be left of her body. The skin would be gone but the hair would still be there. Erin and Savannah were both blondes.

A man yelled, the triumph in his voice almost obscene. *Oh, God. They've found something.*

Gunner whined and licked her left cheek, then the right. Odd, since he never licked both sides. At least she had an excuse for her wet face. She accepted she was crying because the men on the bank and whatever body they were pulling out had blurred and it was no longer possible to see.

Then someone squeezed her shoulder and Justin's voice whispered in her ear: "It's Savannah. The divers are going to keep looking but there doesn't seem to be anyone else down there. Do you want to leave now?"

She nodded, unable to speak, overcome by a wave of sadness along with guilty relief that it wasn't Erin.

"Okay," Justin said. "Follow the same path we took in, until you're outside the marked perimeter. My driver will pick you up in a black Jeep and take you to the command post. Wait there. I need you to sign some forms and get an imprint of your boots."

She gave another nod, somewhat relieved she and Gunner wouldn't have to battle through the thick brush to her car. But Justin would have to wait for forensics and the coroner, and she didn't want to hang around. She just wanted to go home where it was safe to let out her feelings.

Justin had already turned away, striding back to that sad sodden body with the dripping water and tangled hair.

"Let's go, Gunner," she whispered, taking his ball and dropping it into her pack.

She followed the fluorescent ribbons tied to the branches, copying Justin's purposeful stride. Gunner's solid presence helped her walk a bit straighter. A woman in a reflective vest and muddy hiking boots rushed over and raised the yellow tape.

"Good job," she said.

Nikki ducked beneath the tape, forcing a nod. It didn't feel like a good job. Clearly Gunner preferred a different outcome as well. He alternately sniffed at the ground then looked at her face, as if asking for another chance.

She tugged off her plastic booties and reached over to unbuckle his tracking harness. She should have removed the harness earlier, help him get out of work mentality. He was still trying to please her, picking up on everyone's gloomy mood and eager to fix it.

Of course, it didn't have to be tragic for Gunner. He could end the day on a high note if she let him run the track to the barn. Back to Savannah's living, breathing horse.

She clipped the line back on his harness, causing Gunner's tail to swing. He was already sniffing at a hoof print, whining and quivering with eagerness. "Please cancel my Jeep ride," Nikki said to the woman in the vest. "We'll walk out."

Then she turned to Gunner. "Find!" she said.

Twenty minutes later, she and Gunner burst from the trail head onto the gravel lot on the south side of the stable. The parking lot was still crammed with vehicles but now a coroner's van and forensic teams had joined the police cruisers.

A bay horse in a nearby paddock lifted his head, eyeing her curiously before returning to munching hay. It was a beautiful day but most of the turnouts were empty. No doubt, stable activity had been reduced to a minimum, with entry restricted to the owners and essential staff. Gunner didn't look sideways. He tugged her past the paddocks, his nose skimming the ground, intent on following the Arabian's trail.

They swept into the cool confines of the barn where she was hit with a blast of déjà vu. She and Erin had pushed countless wheelbarrows down the long aisle, and she remembered every inch. There were a few aesthetic improvements and others designed for the comfort of the horses: window boxes of colorful daisies, thick rubber in the aisles and expensive cooling fans mounted at regular intervals. And then, in front of the sixth stall to the left, Gunner dropped to his haunches, tail swinging in triumph.

She shoved away her nostalgia, focusing on the light gray horse who'd poked his head over the door, curious about the big dog sitting by his stall. The gelding wore a black leather halter with a plaque proclaiming he'd covered five hundred trail miles. He had a white mane, an elegant head and a prominent dip above his nose—clearly an Arabian. His brown eyes were large and expressive. Whoever had dumped Savannah in the murky water, whatever had happened beside that deserted quarry, this horse had been a witness. And it wasn't the first time Nikki wished an animal could talk.

She pulled Gunner's ball from her pack. Despite the horrors of the day, this time she was determined to properly reward him.

"Good boy," she said. "You found him."

However, it was hard to fake enthusiasm with an astute dog like Gunner. His ears drooped and he caught the ball with a distinct lack of gusto.

"Good boy!" she repeated, forcing a happy singsong voice.

"What's happened?" a man called. The light from the end of the barn reduced him to a silhouette and she could only make out the outline of his ball cap and a sturdy wheelbarrow. "Do you want to check Savannah's horse again?"

The man left the wheelbarrow and hurried toward her. He carried a pitchfork but wore light khakis and low leather shoes, an odd choice for mucking out stalls.

"I can tie Scooter in the aisle," the man said, giving an agreeable smile. "In case you want to check the dirt on his legs again. I already gave the detective Savannah's log book. Like I said earlier, she was covering a lot of territory, trying to hit a thousand miles by December."

"No, thanks," Nikki said, hiding her wince. But it wasn't her place to reveal that they'd be bringing Savannah out in a body bag and that the rescue had turned into a murder investigation. This man clearly thought she was part of the official search team, and the fact that he was the only person in the barn indicated he was staff or an owner.

"Savannah was one of our first boarders," the man said, tugging at his ball cap. "She always cleaned Scooter's stall too. My staff loved her."

So he was the owner. That might explain his inappropriate footwear. Nikki turned toward the door, hoping to avoid any questions about the search, questions she had no authority to answer.

"Savannah loved riding those groomed trails that the previous people had cleared," the owner went on. "She was so proud of her little horse. Scooter isn't much of a jumper but he's an Arabian so has tons of stamina. I imagine she just rode a little too far yesterday, fell off and is stuck somewhere..." His voice quavered and Nikki felt something tear at her chest. She knew what it was like to be on the outside, waiting for news.

Compassion made her pause in the aisle. "When did you buy the stable?" she asked, gently guiding him to a safer topic.

"Six years ago. It took a while to get the place going but now my wife and I have a waiting list for stalls. Some private schools have even incorporated lessons as part of their program. That's been a big boost."

Nikki gave a congratulatory nod. Business had taken a hit after Erin's disappearance and though she remained ambivalent about this barn and especially its trail rides, she'd once genuinely loved the stable. She gave herself an extra moment to inhale the sweet smell of alfalfa. Being around horses again was bittersweet yet she couldn't stop herself from savoring the sights and sounds.

"I used to come here when I was a kid," she said, her voice rusty.

The man brightened. He was actually quite good looking when he smiled, if one liked that clean preppy look. She didn't.

"Some of the horses were included when we bought the property," he said. "We still have a couple of the jumpers. Maybe you'd remember them?"

"I wasn't a boarder," Nikki said. "And I never graduated from the ponies."

"Ponies are strict teachers," he said with a chuckle. "We have one here that is tougher than any of the big horses. Stormy has taught a lot of kids to sit deep, or else they'll find themselves face-first in the dirt."

"Stormy?" Nikki had been edging toward the door but now she jerked around. "He's still here?"

"Sure. He's in the little run-in by the staff parking lot. We don't have enough stalls for boarders so our own horses stay outside." He stuck out his hand. "I'm Matthew Friedel."

"I'm Nikki," she said, shaking his hand. "And I'd love to see Stormy."

"This way." Matthew happily set down his pitchfork and gestured toward the far door. "By the way, if you ever want to drop by for a trail ride, I'm offering the police and search teams a reduced rate."

Matthew was a born salesman and he walked uncomfortably close, his hand nearly grazing her hip. She didn't like people in her personal space and she would never ride again—not without Erin. But she definitely wanted to see Stormy before she left.

She shot Matthew a look, and he shrugged and eased away. It was fortunate Gunner still wore his tracking harness. He was more accepting of strange men when he was in work mode. And though he was eyeing Matthew, he looked more disappointed than protective. No doubt, he'd been anticipating some fun ball play after successfully tracking Savannah's horse.

Nikki teasingly tugged at the ball in Gunner's mouth and he squeezed his jaws, happy with the attention. Matthew didn't even notice their little game. He walked beside her, proudly pointing out all the improvements he and his wife had made and how they'd even added superfast WiFi in the viewing lounge.

"Teens like to hang out," he went on, "so we have an open door policy. Bring a guest and let them see what horses are all about. Some of them come and never ride. But they might tell a friend."

Numerous padded chairs and charging stations supported that it was indeed a welcoming place. Savannah's killer might have visited her at the barn, even sat in one of those colorful armchairs. The impression of a blanket suggested she hadn't been killed by a stranger. Unfortunately with such a wide range of visitors, police would be swamped with interviews.

Gunner bumped her fisted hand, questioning why she wasn't throwing his ball. Justin had stressed that if she kept the rewards consistent, he'd never lose his training. She hadn't done a good job of that today.

"Is there a place by the turnouts where I could throw my dog's ball?" she asked, cutting off Matthew as he rambled on about the shock cushioning of the black rubber mats.

"Certainly," he said. "The only animals outside are the ones my wife and I own. There won't be any in the outdoor arena or in the paddocks by the staff parking lot." He pointed. "Except for Stormy."

At first Nikki only saw a sun-bleached wooded turnout. Then a tail swished, drawing her attention. A pony stood by the wall of the turnout and other than some graying around his muzzle, Stormy hadn't changed. Even his forelock was the same: scruffy, long, and almost covering his tiny ears.

"Oh wow, he's ageless." She hurried to the fence, knowing he wouldn't remember her. Countless children had come and gone in his life. But it was heartwarming to see how he'd thrived. Clearly he was accustomed to commotion; he barely looked at her and Matthew, remaining in his shaded spot by the shelter.

She gave a low whistle, the sound she used to make whenever she brought him an apple. Amazingly his head lifted, his ears pricking. He stepped out from the shade and ambled toward her, eyes bright with interest.

The fact that he remembered her, or more correctly her whistle, was completely humbling. She hadn't expected that. Unfortunately she had nothing in her pockets except dog treats.

She quickly plucked a handful of grass growing outside the paddock. There wasn't a blade of green left in his turnout so hopefully he'd be satisfied with her offering. Seconds later, the pony stuck his head between the top and middle rail and accepted the grass. He even paused his chewing to give Gunner a welcoming sniff, as if happy to meet a big dog.

Matthew's eyes widened. "He sure remembers you. Usually he's hard to catch. Maybe he's tired of teaching kids to ride. Feel free to go in the paddock and visit. Stormy is bossy with horses but he's good with dogs."

Clearly Gunner was good with Stormy too. He dropped his precious ball at the pony's feet, as if hoping Stormy would throw it. Nikki unclipped the lead from Gunner's harness and slipped beneath the rails. She'd shared many wonderful times with the beloved pony and he'd taught her a lot. Justin had always said if she could earn Stormy's respect, she'd have accomplished something few people ever had.

She scratched the pony's thick neck, his shoulder and the ever-itchy spot beneath his forelock, remembering the first time he'd dumped her in the brook. Justin had laughed, and she'd been so upset. But anger never worked with Stormy, and she'd learned to control her emotions and think like a horse. Or more aptly like an irascible little pony. Three months later, she'd been able to jump Stormy with just a halter, and she wasn't sure who had been more proud—her or Justin.

She glanced toward the path, wondering if he knew the old pony was still here. Maybe Justin would show up soon and they could enjoy this tiny bright spot on such a tragic day. But other than the cluster of vehicles by a large trailer—obviously the command post—there was little movement.

"If you don't mind," she said, glancing at Matthew, "I'm going to stay here for a bit."

It would be a chance to hang out with Stormy again, and the smooth open area would be a great place to throw Gunner's ball. He'd been asked to find two targets today: Savannah and then her horse, and it was important to let him know he'd finished the job. Otherwise Gunner would keep searching, driven by his powerful work ethic, forever looking for a way to please.

"No problem," Matthew said. "Do you have any idea when I'll be allowed to re-open?"

She shook her head and scooped up Gunner's ball, ready to turn her attention to her deserving dog. Except Gunner was no longer in the paddock or by the fence. She wheeled, scanning the adjacent turnouts, hoping he hadn't wandered toward the road.

"Your dog's okay," Matthew said, gesturing at the lone car in the employee lot. "He's sitting down. Probably tired from sniffing around all those trails."

Nikki slipped the ball back in her pack, straining to see Gunner. The dog could move fast but he rarely left her side, not unless he was on a job. And he hadn't wandered far. It was his stillness that made him hard to see, his coat camouflaged against the dusty brown car. Only his tail moved.

Her eyes narrowed. She'd unclipped Gunner's lead but hadn't removed his tracking harness. Obviously he was still in work mode, still searching. And judging by the way he was sitting, he'd found something.

CHAPTER EIGHT

"WHOSE CAR IS THAT?" Nikki asked, careful to keep her voice neutral.

Matthew gave a deprecatory laugh. "Mine. Just an old Ford beater I use. It's better on gas than the truck." He turned, peering over her head toward the trees. "Sounds like some engines coming out. Wonder if they found her."

"Seems unlikely," she said, studying his expression. "You know...considering the distance she always rode."

"That's right. She could be as far as twenty miles out. I gave searchers a map of the area. Pointed out all her regular trails."

"Did she ever ride to the quarry?"

Matthew jerked back, his eyes widening. "No way. That's a dead end, very rocky. All our boarders are warned to avoid the east side. Sharp rocks are too hard on the horses' feet."

"It wasn't a place we rode either," Nikki said.

Matthew nodded, his shoulders relaxing. "I'm sure Savannah took the north trail. No doubt Scooter spooked and threw her. There are a lot of hikers out there, making sudden noises, not realizing how easily they can scare a horse. I just hope they find her soon."

"I'm sure they will," Nikki said, angling away from him. She spotted a black Jeep leading a line of four-wheelers and stepped forward, waving her arms. The Jeep curled away from the search and rescue vehicles, and sped toward her.

The driver stopped the Jeep close to the paddock and cut the engine. Justin unfolded from the passenger's side. His grim expression softened when he spotted the pony. "Well, I'll be dammed," he said. "It's Stormy. And that rascal hasn't aged much."

He reached over the rail and gave the pony an affectionate scratch beneath his jaw. "Just let me know when you're ready to go, Nikki," he said over his shoulder. "I need you to sign some forms and get that imprint. Then I'll have someone drive you to your car."

"Did you find Savannah?" Matthew asked. "Are you checking the old jumper trails?"

Justin silenced him with a flat stare and looked back at Nikki. "You'll be compensated for your work today," he said. "Where's Gunner?"

"That's what I wanted you to see." She gestured at the beige Ford. "Gunner's been sitting like that for several minutes. It's Matthew's car."

"Sir," Justin said, whipping toward Matthew. "Do you mind opening your trunk."

It wasn't a question and Nikki caught the warning look Justin shot the officer sitting behind the wheel of the Jeep. The officer stepped out, his hand hovering over the gun on his hip.

"Why?" Matthew frowned and tugged at his ball cap. "There's nothing in there but horse stuff."

"Then I'm sure you won't mind us having a quick look," Justin said.

Shrugging, Matthew walked toward the car. Gunner rose and pawed at the trunk, impatient to show them what he'd found and delighted to have roused some attention. Nikki clipped on his leash, watching with bated breath.

Matthew reached down and pressed the release. The trunk slowly lifted.

It seemed anti-climatic. The space was surprisingly clean, containing only an old brush, a pair of well-worn boots and a horse blanket. Certainly nothing that seemed to belong to Savannah. But Gunner whined and leaped forward, paws on the bumper, his nose twitching.

Nikki tugged him to the side of the car but not before she spotted the white hairs that stood out in stark contrast against the blue of the blanket.

"Who owns that horse blanket?" Justin asked.

"One of the boarders," Matthew said. "I'm just taking it in for repairs."

Justin said nothing, just leveled his hard stare on Matthew.

"It actually belonged to Savannah," Matthew added, flustered and speaking faster now. "But that doesn't mean anything. It's a service I do for all the boarders."

"Very kind of you." Justin smiled, but his teeth gleamed like a shark's. "Naturally we'll send the blanket to forensics."

Matthew froze, the color seeping from his face. He opened his mouth then closed it again, all the while staring in horror at the blanket. No doubt it contained bodily fluids. He would have been smarter to hide it in the woods. And he'd said "belonged," making it more than the first time he'd referred to Savannah in the past tense. Nikki would have bet her modest bank account that the boots in the trunk matched the tread Justin had noted beside the water.

She pulled Gunner away from the car and kneeled beside him, cradling his head, her throat too tight for words. The thought of Savannah's grieving family left her gutted. But at least they'd have closure. And this time she was going to give her dog the ball game he deserved. And she was going to do it now.

She trudged away from the officer's voice reciting Matthew his rights, pulled out Gunner's ball and threw it in the grassy space beside the paddock. Stormy was silent company, sticking his head between the rails and watching intently as Gunner sped after the ball. The pony remained beside the fence even as three unmarked cruisers sped up, surrounding Matthew and his car.

Nikki focused on throwing Gunner's ball, determined to let him know his job was done. And done well. Savannah's family would be devastated at the news but at least they wouldn't face a lifetime wondering if their daughter would ever return.

Gunner was panting and happy, his tongue lolling when he finally flopped at her feet. But he remained alert. His ears shot forward, locking on someone approaching behind her.

Tony walked up, carrying a bucket of water in one hand and a clipboard and several Power Bars in the other. "I thought the hero of the day might be thirsty," he said, setting the bucket down on the grass for Gunner. "If you ever want to sell him, the K-9 unit would be delighted to have him back. We shouldn't have let this guy go."

Nikki gave a vehement headshake. "No way," she said. "I can't imagine life without him. Are those the forms Justin mentioned?"

"Yes, along with our standard waiver."

"Seems a little late for signing waivers."

"It sure is," Tony said, cheerfully extracting a pen and handing it over. "Good thing you didn't break a leg. But we also have a confidentiality agreement. Justin set you up to be paid a K-9 consulting fee. Admittedly I thought it was a waste, that you and your dog would just get in our way. But Gunner not only found Savannah, he nailed her killer. Justin already has the creep singing like a canary."

Nikki flipped through the forms, signing quickly, acting nonchalant about the generous number handwritten at the bottom of the page. She was making more money in one day than she'd made in the last month. There was also a performance bonus that might kick in. In fact, Justin's heavy scrawl already showed his approval, along with Tony's signature as coordinator of the K-9 units.

"When did he ask you to approve this?"

"This morning," Tony said. "Right after he called you."

She passed back the signed papers, nodding as if she understood Tony's statement. But Justin hadn't phoned her, and she never expected to be made part of the official search. Somehow Justin had known she would come, that she would find a way to circumvent posted security. And the fact that he understood her so well was as comforting as it was disturbing.

"I know this was a tough day," Tony went on. "There's nothing more rewarding than finding a live person. Nothing more gut wrenching than finding a corpse. But I'm glad you came. We needed a dog that could distinguish between the scents of the individual horses and none of our available K-9s could do that. I want to add you and Gunner to our consult list. With your permission of course."

"Of course," she said, her delight at his offer tempered by the thought of Savannah.

"Then it looks like we'll be seeing a lot more of each other." Tony's blue eyes twinkled. "Maybe you'll even visit the K-9 center before our open house in the fall."

She gave a smiling nod, keen to watch their training exercises and see some other working dogs. It would be a pleasure to be around people who understood police animals. They wouldn't try to be best friends with Gunner and turn frustrated at his reserve. Or worse, get into her space too quickly, something the last guy she'd dated had discovered.

Tony was obviously a dog person though, remaining a polite distance away, shoulders relaxed and hands at his sides. Gunner seemed to accept him as non-threatening. Maybe he even remembered Tony from his time at the center. In fact, Gunner dropped his ball, nosing it forward several inches, inviting him to play. Tony kneeled and rolled the ball back. Gunner gave a tiny tail wag and nosed it forward again.

And soon Gunner was lying on his back, letting Tony rub his vulnerable belly, relaxed as a family pet. And Nikki's heart warmed like a mother watching her child.

"He likes you," she said. "Hard to believe he can be aggressive."

"Everyone likes me if they give me a chance." Tony's cocky grin was belied by the twinkle in his eye. "And Gunner's real failing was that he refused to climb. Nothing would motivate him. I'll dig out his file. Maybe he had an excuse. Perhaps his hind end is weak."

Nikki dropped to her knees, staring in dismay at her dog's hips. Justin had mentioned Gunner's inability to climb but she hadn't realized it might be health related. She'd read many troubling stories about German Shepherds and hip dysplasia. Now though, life without him was unimaginable.

Her mind scrambled over the scenarios. There must be ways to compensate. If Gunner faced mobility issues she'd buy a little wagon. That way she could pull him and he'd still be able to join her on their daily runs. He'd probably be unhappy though, especially at Sonja's. Seeing all the farm animals and not being able to track and play would be heartbreaking.

"Hey," Tony said, his voice empathetic. "I'm sure he's fine. I was watching him today and he moves well. We have a vet onsite along with a range of strengthening and rehab equipment. If you're worried, come by for a visit. I'll have staff work out an exercise program for him."

"I'd love that," she said. "When's a good day to come?"

"I knew the only way to get a date with you would be through your dog." His accompanying grin was so unabashed she couldn't stop her burst of laughter. Besides, it was refreshing to sit on the grass with a good-looking guy who wasn't petrified of her dog. A man who was thoughtful enough to bring water and energy bars.

She chewed on the bars, entranced as Tony talked animatedly about the training center. Despite his jokes, police dogs were obviously his passion and it was all so interesting she didn't realize they were no longer alone, not until a figure behind her cast a towering shadow.

CHAPTER NINE

"YOU TWO ARE MAKING this look like a Sunday afternoon picnic," Justin snapped, ice in his voice.

Nikki scrambled to her feet, her smile fading. She'd been so engrossed in Tony's K-9 tales, she hadn't noticed Justin's approach. And Gunner had been relaxed too, completely accepting of Tony, letting him rub his jaws even when they were wrapped around his treasured ball.

"Just getting to know the hero of the hour," Tony said, giving Gunner an approving pat. "Both of them," he added, turning his smile back to Nikki.

She had to give him top marks for courage. Most people wilted beneath Justin's displeasure. But Tony was still smiling as he scooped up the clipboard. "See you soon, Nikki," he called over his shoulder, giving her an irreverent wink before sauntering away.

She gave a weak nod, aghast that she'd been sprawled on the grass, temporarily forgetting about the day's grisly find.

"I don't mind you socializing," Justin said, his mouth tight. "Just not this close to a crime scene. The optics aren't good."

They weren't visible from the road or the command post but this wasn't the time to be defensive. Besides, he was absolutely right. Robert had always stressed that if she was to develop a successful business, she needed to be aware of every social nuance. To care a little bit more about rules and norms instead of charging forward. Besides, in addition to Justin's annoyance, he also looked concerned. No doubt he'd been meticulously building a case, trying to keep everything airtight before Matthew Friedel lawyered up.

"I'm sorry," she said.

His eyebrow arched. "You've changed. That's one of the few times I've ever heard you apologize."

She kept herself from wincing but they both remembered her first apology. When her sister hadn't returned from that horrible trail ride, she'd blamed him for letting Erin skip barn chores. The accusation had been unfair but Justin's tortured expression remained seared in her brain.

"I'm not a kid anymore," she said. "And I have to stay calm now. Gunner can get really aggressive if he thinks I'm upset."

"He seemed to like Tony well enough," Justin said.

"Tony's great with dogs." She gave a rueful smile. "And it's much easier to be around men when my dog doesn't want to eat them."

Justin chuckled, that deep masculine laugh that always warmed her insides. But they both knew she wasn't joking. There had been more than one occasion when Gunner had nipped—well, actually bit—guys she'd been dating. Once it had been in a man's most vulnerable spot. He'd threatened to report her dog as dangerous until she'd called Justin in a panic. She wasn't sure what Justin had said, but the guy had quietly disappeared.

And it wasn't as though Justin wasn't busy with more important matters. Like Robert, he was one of the rare people she could always depend on.

"Want to stop for a beer?" she asked impulsively. "I'll buy, seeing as you landed me a windfall today."

"Rain check." He raked a hand through his hair. "I'll have an interview back at headquarters once the suspect is processed."

His refusal was disappointing but unsurprising. Lately he seemed to be avoiding her. They'd had drinks together but only when she ran into him and whatever lady he was currently seeing. He never seemed to approve of Nikki's dates and she certainly didn't like his girlfriends, especially since too often they tracked her down afterwards, asking about Justin and wondering why he'd ghosted. Their calls always left her irritated.

"Just ask him," she'd say. Justin was so blunt, she couldn't understand their reluctance or why they thought she'd know anything about his love life. She'd come to accept she was wary of smoothing other people's feelings. She'd done that for Erin and it had made her sister vulnerable and thin-skinned. Being left at the brook would have been devastating for Erin's self-esteem, and no doubt the reason she'd dismounted and tied Pancho to the tree.

At least Nikki could pray that Erin might show up some day. Savannah's family didn't have that faint hope, although it was questionable which was worse. Maybe knowing *was* better.

Gunner whined and she realized she was twisting his lead between her fingers, her agitation running down the leash.

Justin's gaze flickered over her tight fist. "It's been a rough day," he said, his voice softening. "Give me your keys and I'll have someone drive your car home. There's a restaurant close by that allows dogs. I need an imprint of your boots and after that I'll have time to grab a quick bite."

She couldn't help but smile with gratitude. She didn't want to go home alone with her thoughts, and there was no one she'd rather unwind with than Justin. But she really did want a beer.

"Is that restaurant licensed for alcohol?" she asked.

The corners of his mouth curved in understanding. "I believe so. And if not, I'm sure we can convince them to bring you one."

Forty minutes later, they were seated in the restaurant and an efficient, gray-haired waitress was sliding plates and a soup bowl across the vinyl tablecloth.

Nikki sipped her cold beer, sighing with appreciation. Justin had snagged a booth in the back where Gunner had plenty of room to lie at their feet. Once staff realized they'd been involved in the local search, they welcomed Gunner, even bringing him a big bowl of water. Best of all, Gunner was relaxed, not eyeing every man around with open suspicion. He seemed to think Justin was a worthy protector.

"This is perfect," she said.

"It's just a greasy diner," Justin said. "But yes, this is perfect."

There was an odd note in his voice and she glanced up, wondering if he was laughing at her. She suspected he preferred high-end establishments and glamorous dates, not someone who preferred to wear jeans and a T-shirt. But there was no mockery in his expression and his smile was almost wistful. He was likely starving since he had two huge steaks in front of him along with a plate of golden-brown fries that looked and smelled delicious.

"Try some fries," he said, pushing the plate to the middle of the table. "They're some of the best around."

She'd eaten a protein bar with Tony and under the circumstances hadn't expected to be able to stomach a big meal. But Justin had made an appealing mound of salt and ketchup so she picked up a fry, dipped it, and took a nibble. Her eyes widened. He wasn't exaggerating. The fry was delicious: hot and crunchy on the outside but light and fluffy in the center.

"How did you know they'd be so good?" she asked, alternating now between sips of her beer and his fries, wishing she'd ordered them instead of her watery chicken soup.

"I used to eat here," he said. "Back when I was working at the stable."

"That's right. I remember you often left muffins in the tack room. Erin and I were always hungry. There was one kind she liked that no one else ate so she always got double."

"Banana and chocolate chip."

She paused, a fry halfway to her mouth, astonished he remembered. There had been a lot of kids around. Of course, Justin had a razor-sharp memory to go with his brilliant detective mind. She had no doubt he'd nail Matthew Friedel to the cross. Robert had confided that over the last few years Justin had achieved a ninety percent closure rate. Obviously Justin couldn't say much about this case but it was impossible not to dwell on Savannah. And while Nikki had worked hard to smooth her impulsive nature, it was natural to ask him questions.

"Why do you think Matthew killed her?" she said.

Justin took a sip of coffee, the muscles of his tanned throat rippling. He seemed to be debating about how much to reveal. "He probably didn't plan to," he finally said.

She nibbled on the tip of another golden fry. Matthew had obviously been meeting Savannah for some time, judging by the amount of horse manure piled around the tree. And he'd deliberately misled the searchers, sending them to the north and hoping they wouldn't find her body. DNA analysis of the blanket would likely show they'd been having sex. Perhaps Savannah had threatened to tell his wife.

But was that enough reason to kill someone?

"Killers have different motivations," Justin said. "At the time, they can be overpowering."

She must have voiced the question aloud or else, as usual, Justin had guessed her thoughts. And though she understood he couldn't talk about the case except in generalities, it was impossible to tamp down her anger. A girl's life had been snuffed. And Savannah's family would never be the same.

"Matthew wasn't even upset," she said, angrily jabbing her fry into the white mound on Justin's plate. "Only worried when his riding business could re-open. And he spoke about Savannah in the past tense. What a creep."

"You won't meet the cream of society in this business," Justin said, pulling away his plate so she couldn't keep layering her fry in salt. "Is that what turned you on to him? How he talked about her in the past tense?"

"That and his shoes. It was as if he'd searched for the smallest ones in his closet. And it didn't make sense he wasn't wearing practical barn boots."

"Very observant." Justin gave an approving nod. "You did excellent work today, you and Gunner. And he deserves a reward."

He lifted the steak from his second plate, slipping it beneath the table, and it was then she realized why he'd ordered two meals. She peered beneath the table, smiling as Gunner gulped down the boneless meat. She never fed him from the table but Justin made his own rules and obviously he still had a soft spot for Gunner. Besides, her dog did deserve a steak.

"By the way," she said, straightening in her chair. "Tony mentioned you paid a lot of money for Gunner. I thought he flunked out because of the climbing problem. But Tony said the protection unit could have used him, even though he was turning aggressive. Why did you give him to me?"

"You and Tony certainly found a lot to talk about," Justin said, jamming his knife into the last piece of steak.

She'd learned from long experience when he didn't intend to answer her questions. Generally it was because he thought she should work out the answer on her own. But lately he was becoming even more difficult to read.

"Some day I'll pay you back," she said, reaching across the table and touching his wrist. "I didn't realize you'd spent money on Gunner. But I'll be forever grateful."

Justin stiffened and she quickly moved her hand away, pretending she was going for the last fry.

"I didn't want him stuck in riot control," Justin said. "That's no place for a nice dog like him."

She nodded in total agreement. Compliments about Gunner were always welcomed. And the beer, along with Justin's company, had left her unusually mellow.

"Yes," she said. "He's much too nice for that. And I really don't mind that he's aggressive with men."

Justin looked up from his plate, his eyes glinting. "Neither do I," he said.

CHAPTER TEN

NIKKI SETTLED DEEPER into the car seat, relaxing against the comfortable headrest. Justin was excellent company and he always drove an understated but powerful vehicle. If the day had started at the restaurant, she would have considered it a wonderful day. Any time with him was well spent. But it didn't seem right that she felt so warm and mellow while Savannah wasn't able to feel a thing.

Justin always knew how to soothe her though. She remembered every one of his pep talks, from the time Stormy had dumped her in the brook to when she'd been overwhelmed in Japan, believing she'd never complete her martial arts certification.

She turned her head, studying his chiseled profile. The sun had lowered but the glow from the dashboard revealed his half smile. Clearly the restaurant break had left him content as well, rather amazing considering the fact that he and his partner would soon be grilling a killer.

She gave a pensive sigh. "How do you deal with all the sadness? Case after case? Days like this?"

His clipped shrug spoke volumes and she realized he wasn't as unaffected as he appeared. It took a moment for him to answer.

"I compartmentalize," he said, his voice as gruff as it had been that long ago day when an abandoned kitten has been run over by a car. He'd sent her inside to brush Stormy so she didn't have to see the tiny broken body. But she'd felt his sorrow, had spotted him reverently burying the animal, and the knowledge that he was similarly moved had been as comforting then as it was now.

"I try not to get too close to the victims," he went on. "Or their families. Sometimes it's a struggle."

"I feel guilty when I forget." Her candid admission surprised her. Blocking emotion had always been her way of coping with pain. But being at the stable had stirred up a variety of feelings, many of them not good.

"We'll always be shaped by Erin." He reached over and squeezed her knee. "There's no way around it."

She couldn't remember the last time he'd touched her like that, and she clutched at his hand, keeping it close, needing the warm contact. "Do you think she's still alive?"

He turned his wrist and now he was the one holding her hand, calm and comforting. "No," he said. "No, I don't."

Hearing that from others always left her feeling angry. Betrayed. But it was different coming from Justin. She even remained composed enough to voice the haunting question, one that left her nights sleepless and her bed sheets a tangled mess. "Do you think she's buried back there?" she asked. "Somewhere near that horse property?"

"I haven't looked at the file lately. But I had a cadaver dog in there. Found nothing."

"I didn't know you'd done that." Her leg twitched in reaction, picturing him trudging through those dense lonely woods, hoping he'd find Erin—hoping he wouldn't.

"It was one of the first things I did when I made detective."

She wanted to thank him but her throat had thickened and she didn't trust herself to speak. She pressed down on her restless leg, trying to still the movement as she blinked out the side window. All this time she'd thought the police had forgotten, that they'd shoved Erin in the cold case drawer. Even Robert rarely discussed her now that most of his contacts had retired. But Justin hadn't forgotten. And that knowledge made her feel much less alone.

"Thank you," she finally managed, swallowing back the persistent lump clogging her throat. "Why didn't you tell me?"

"Didn't want to get your hopes up. And you would have been out there, dogging me like a tick when it was more important that you be studying."

"But you knew I'd show up today. You even knew I'd enter by the brook. And you let me stay."

"You're older now. Not so impulsive. Besides, you made a good case for Gunner. He has a good nose and the instincts to go with it. His foundation training was excellent. It was a no-brainer."

He sounded defensive, as if justifying the decision, and she sensed he would have let her stay even without Gunner. As the ranking detective, it had been his call to make.

"I appreciate you letting me stay. You've always been so kind."

"Not something I'm often called," he said dryly.

"But you are." She squeezed his hand then pressed a kiss on the back of his fingers. They were thick and warm with a prickle of hair that tickled her lips, and they smelled good. Fresh and woodsy. She inhaled deeper, catching a hint of fries and something else. The masculine smell she always associated with Justin.

Oh, no. She realized she was sniffing his fingers like an adoring dog and dropped his hand, heat creeping across her cheeks. She'd worked too hard hiding her attraction to let it escape now, in this rare moment of weakness. Luckily her street was the next intersection. It couldn't come quickly enough. Her face was hot, the air in the car stifling. Dammit, her entire body tingled. But she didn't want Justin to guess her feelings.

Behind her, Gunner whined and pressed his nose against the back of her neck, as if checking her temperature. She shifted, pressing her shoulder against the door.

"It's the next turn, second duplex on the right," she muttered, even as he cut the wheel. Of course he knew where she lived. He'd been there several times. Had installed Gunner's dog door.

His vehicle jerked to a stop in front of her house. Uncharacteristic for a driver of Justin's caliber. Normally she would have teased him about driving like a teenager, but her lips felt thick and all she wanted was to escape, to hide from his astute eyes. She fumbled for her seatbelt even as he swung open the driver's door.

"Stay, Gunner," he said, stepping out.

Seconds later, he opened her door, tugged her out and shifted her against the fender. He stared at her face for a long moment, as if conflicted. Then his eyes locked on her lips and his mouth lowered, covering hers, leaving her too shocked to move. But the inertia only lasted a second. Because she'd been imagining, hoping and picturing this kiss for years and she knew what she wanted.

She rose on her toes, wrapped her arms around his neck and kissed him back. By the time he lifted his head, she was breathless with want.

"Are you finally ready for me?" he asked, his voice gravely.

She didn't understand his question. He must know she was ready. Her leg was twined around the back of his calf, her hand tucked beneath his shirt, and she couldn't stop her fingers from running over those warm ridged muscles. She'd admired them in the gym before, all shiny, strong and sweaty. But she'd never been able to touch them—not the way his girlfriends did—and all she could do was stare up at him in a mix of shock and desire.

He swore, but it was the sexiest, gentlest curse she'd ever heard him use, and then he was kissing her again, his lips back over hers but this time his tongue moved inside her mouth with a dominating sweep. Warmth melted through her, reaching her very core.

Way too soon, he lifted his mouth, his hand cupping the back of her head, his eyes a question.

"Wow," she whispered, gratified by the relief that played across his face. But if the way he kissed was an indicator of the other things he did, she understood why all his girlfriends wanted him back. She certainly didn't want him distancing himself from her. But a month together, heck, even one night, might be worth it. She wasn't a fan of long relations anyway.

She still couldn't believe she was wrapped in his arms, her fingers beneath his shirt, free to explore whatever part of that body she wanted... Then it hit her: He wasn't touching her anywhere except with his mouth. As usual, she was the one who was recklessly forging ahead. Clearly he didn't share her urgency.

"Guess we had a little too much to drink," she said, forcing a laugh, giving him a way out even though they both knew he'd sipped nothing but coffee.

He dragged his thumb over her lower lip. "We're not going backwards with this, Nik."

He hadn't called her Nik in a long time and certainly never with such a bedroom voice. Frankly she wanted him in her bed, and there seemed no good reason to keep denying it. "Then let's go inside," she said.

He splayed a hand around the back of her neck, the touch of his fingers creating another delightful rush of sensation. "I can't stay," he sighed. "Not tonight."

It seemed his touch had totally wiped away the knowledge that he was waiting on warrants. And he needed to be sharp for the interview. Needed to make sure he didn't slip up, for Savannah's sake.

"Of course you can't stay." She pushed her arms to her side and stepped back. "Go and nail that creep. I'll see you when you're free."

"Yes," he said, his gaze holding hers. "You will."

Succinct, but there was a wealth of meaning in his words, and her heart gave an ecstatic kick. Because Justin always did what he said, and judging by the way he was devouring her with his eyes he didn't intend to stay away for long.

CHAPTER ELEVEN

———◦———

"CARAMEL MACCHIATO!" Sonja's eyes widened with delight. "You know it's my favorite. But that's extravagant."

"We're celebrating," Nikki said, closing Sonja's door and bobbing her head at Gunner. "He was amazing yesterday."

"I heard about a dog tracking a suspect at some riding stable," Sonja said. "Did you and Gunner help with that?"

"Yes, and we might have a chance to work with the police again. The head of the K-9 teams is adding us to his call list. He's really nice. Even Gunner liked him."

"So that explains your aura today." Sonja's head tilted, her eyes narrowing. "It's different, not so dark. I'm seeing a hot guy, someone you actually want to spend time with."

"Knock it off," Nikki scoffed, taking a quick sip of coffee. She was never certain if Sonja could actually see things. Her friend had been correct on a few occasions, and she would always be grateful that Sonja had convinced her to buy a spare tire, two days before a very inconvenient flat. But tire trouble was in most drivers' futures.

And the only time Nikki had requested Sonja's help with finding Erin, it had been an agonizing waste. She and Robert had pounded the pavement for weeks, talking to every sex worker, spurred by Sonja's vision of Erin surrounded by concrete. Other than meeting some interesting ladies, Sonja's lead had been a total bust. Of course, the fact that Sonja believed Erin was dead had colored the search, and by tacit agreement neither of them discussed her psychic powers again.

Now though, Sonja stared with assessing blue eyes, looking as if she could strip away the protective armor and see the suspicious soul Nikki always kept hidden. "Don't push this guy away," Sonja said softly. "Not everyone will leave you."

"I'm going back to my office if you intend to psychoanalyze me." Nikki softened her words with a smile because she was in an exceptionally good mood. And though Tony was undeniably hot it was Justin who had left her floating on a cloud. Or more honestly, swept away on a rush of lust.

She'd always wondered what it would feel like to be kissed by Justin, and the reality was so much better than the imagining. Her lips tingled just thinking of his touch and she was intensely curious what his next kiss would be like. And where it would undoubtedly lead. However, her relationship with Justin was far too fragile to discuss with anyone, even Sonja.

"Drink your coffee and admire the super dog," Nikki added, still smiling. "He really was awesome."

"Tell me about it." Sonja gave an agreeable nod, deferring with her usual graciousness. "Can you talk about what he did?"

"Not much," Nikki said. "It's confidential and I'm not sure what information the police have released. But I can say that tracking all your farm animals certainly helped. So thank you. And Gunner loves horses. He even licked a gelding's face."

"I'm not surprised," Sonja said. "Beneath that ferocious appearance, he's a real gentleman. He wants everyone to be safe and feels duty bound to make that happen. Especially if it pleases you."

Nikki nodded, impressed at Sonja's accurate assessment. Sometimes her friend said the wisest things.

"But how did you get invited on the case?" Sonja asked. "Did Robert have a contact with this new guy? By the way, that shade of lipstick does amazing things. It's not often you wear a sexy color, not at the office." Sonja's eyes were twinkling now. She might be a psychic fraud but her observational powers were top notch.

"You look stunning," Sonja went on, her approving gaze dropping over Nikki's silky blouse and fitted black pants. "I gather you're expecting company."

"Just Robert," Nikki said. It was doubtful Justin would have any free time over the next couple of days. A detective working a fresh homicide meant endless hours of gathering evidence and chasing a variety of leads. There was no telling when he'd call. But just in case he did drop by, she had taken extra time to dress.

"You didn't put that makeup on for Robert," Sonja said. "And I want to know everything. Not about the case but about the guy that has you looking like a gorgeous runway model."

Nikki made a chopping motion with her hand, rose and headed toward the door, followed closely by Gunner. Justin was still too fresh to share and she hadn't been joking about leaving, if pushed. "An all-seeing psychic shouldn't have to be told anything," she said over her shoulder. "Just look it up in your tea leaves or something."

"If you'd sit still long enough for a reading," Sonja said, "I could do that. Remember, be careful who you trust!"

Nikki pulled the door shut and escaped into the deserted hall. Sonja often told her to be careful but Nikki didn't trust anyone so it was a rather gratuitous warning. People always disappointed her whether it was intentional or not. Erin certainly hadn't planned to disappear. However, her mother and father had made their own decisions. And trusting people, loving them, only led to pain.

She followed Gunner down the hall. He led the way, nose to the floor as he trotted toward her office. Then he sat and waited in front of her door, his all-clear sign apparent. Unlike humans, he was alert even when diligence wasn't required.

"Good dog," she said, pressing in the electronic code and waiting for the beep. At Robert's advice, she'd installed heavy security doors and locks, partly to protect confidential files and also because people could turn downright nasty. She still used the codes but with Gunner around she no longer worried about strangers bursting in, red-faced and arm-waving because an insurance company had voided their claim. Or because a wronged spouse had sued for divorce. Gunner's presence tended to keep everyone calm. Best of all, bill collecting had turned into a breeze.

The only thing he couldn't help her with was surveillance. She could pull on a wig and sunglasses and alter her appearance. But it was impossible to disguise Gunner. And a parked car could quickly turn into a sweltering oven.

Some day she hoped to afford one of the air conditioning units that the K-9 vehicles had. Some had an alarm that signaled when the interior was too warm, along with a button to remotely open the dog's door. And the GPS tracking monitors were very cool, the kind that could measure a dog's temperature and let the handler know if the dog was overheating. Gunner deserved that. And more.

Perhaps if she could land more police contracts, her business would finally take off. That type of work would certainly be more fulfilling. Despite the horror of finding Savannah's body, helping to nab a killer left her with a heady sense of accomplishment, not to mention that Savannah's family would have a level of closure. Right now, that probably didn't matter much to them. But down the road it would. She knew that for a fact.

She pushed open the door and plunked down behind her desk. After the highs and lows of yesterday, returning to her current caseload wasn't very motivating. She didn't care if Steven Foster had wrenched his back making on-the-job deliveries or if Anita Harrington was really screwing her muscle-bound chauffeur.

She wanted to help people in a more significant way. And after Gunner's tracking success yesterday, her mission to find Erin's abductor had risen back to the forefront.

She powered on her laptop and scrolled over the latest news. Savannah's face was everywhere. Nikki didn't want to read the human interest reports detailing the girl's academic achievements—straight 'A's' except a C in history. Or how Savannah had won three blue ribbons at a state horse show and taught her little brother to swim. It was too close to Erin's story and only scraped the wounds buried deep in Nikki's chest. Even so, it seemed disrespectful to ignore the details of such a tragically shortened life.

So she read every word, aching for Savannah, her family and her friends, barely aware that Gunner had pressed his head on her lap, trying to absorb her pain.

The door clicked open. "Hey," Robert's empathetic voice said. "Bad time?"

She kept a box of tissues on her desk for upset clients and now she snatched one, blotting her eyes before glancing up. "I'm fine," she murmured, clearing her throat. "Come in," she called, her voice more assertive.

Robert had seen her cry a few times before, the first when she'd flipped over the front of Erin's too-big tricycle and smashed her nose, the last when her sister had disappeared. He knew she rarely indulged in tears. Luckily it wasn't Justin who had dropped by her office. He might not let her help on police cases again if he saw the raw emotion they dredged up.

"I was afraid a missing rider would bring back nightmares," Robert said, his forehead creased with worry. "But I have information that might make you feel better. This case bears no similarity to Erin's. They retrieved the victim's body yesterday. The killer is a slam-dunk. In fact, he already confessed."

Nikki kept her expression impassive but her fingers squeezed the tissue, turning it into a soggy ball. So Matthew Friedel wasn't fighting the charge. How fortunate for the family that there would be no dragged-out court case. Naturally Robert had no idea she and Gunner had been allowed to help in the search. Or that she'd driven out to the stable against his advice.

"The victim and the stable owner had been having an affair," Robert went on. "She was pregnant and when she told him, he panicked. Strangled her and hid her body in some quarry runoff."

Nikki leaned back against the chair, her hands fisted below the desk. Robert's information was always bang-on. He'd been a police officer for nearly twenty years and still had reliable sources deep in the department. The fact that Savannah was pregnant explained why Matthew had been so desperate to hide her body. DNA evidence would point directly to him. He'd probably copped a plea in exchange for a lesser charge. The scumball might be out in less than twenty years while Savannah's life had been snuffed.

"It wasn't an affair," she said.

"My sources are quite certain."

"You can't call it an affair," she snapped, driving the ball of tissue into the trash can with a jarring plunk. "Savannah was sixteen, an impressionable kid. That creep took advantage of his power and position. He preyed on her!"

A red stain climbed Robert's neck and she immediately regretted her burst of emotion. He'd called in a favor, then hurried over with the news, hoping to make her feel better. He was the last person she'd ever want to hurt.

She pulled in a calming breath before speaking again. "It's just that Savannah was a horse nut. She didn't care about boys and she wasn't a consenting adult—"

"You're right." Robert raised his palms in agreement. "It definitely wasn't an affair and I apologize. Even though I mentored you myself, I sometimes forget your legal training. And as usual the killer was someone close to the victim. If only it was this simple back with Erin."

"It would have made things easier," Nikki said. "But the barn owners were a lovely gay couple who Erin and I barely knew."

"They were out of state then too." Robert sank into the chair, giving a resigned sigh. "At first I thought your friend Justin Decker was good for it. So did your mom. We remembered Erin's flirting and how he acted around her."

"Wait..." Nikki froze, her hands re-clenching on her lap. "What do you mean? How did he act?"

Certainly all the older girls had been infatuated with Justin, trying countless ways to gain his attention. The shyer ones had simply blushed when he strode past; the bolder girls had tried a variety of tricks. But unless it was a horse question, he never responded. And he'd fired the stable worker who kept dressing inappropriately.

"Justin never spoke much," Nikki went on. "Only when he was teaching. Or if someone wasn't treating a horse properly. He didn't encourage flirting. In fact, he never seemed to notice that sort of thing."

"Oh, he noticed all right." Robert's mouth flattened into a disapproving line. "Erin was a beautiful girl. Your mother always fretted about her clothes and how she insisted on showing off her figure, especially at the barn."

Nikki rubbed her forehead. That was true. Erin had worn tight breeches even when she mucked out stalls. She remembered worrying that her sister might start wearing a skimpy top too. She hadn't realized Erin had been trying to get Justin's attention, had thought she was just copying the older girls.

"I remember the tight breeches," she said slowly. "But I never understood the reason. I thought it was all about fitting in with the boarders."

"That's because you were focused on the horses. Your father had a singular focus like that too. And he was just as stubborn. When Paul met your mother she was dating someone else. One thing for sure, he wasn't a quitter."

Nikki's expression turned stony and Robert clamped his mouth shut, realizing he'd made a mistake. The office was silent except for the whirring of the air conditioner.

"Sorry," Robert finally said, his voice gruff. "Guess he did quit. I know you don't like to hear about your dad but he was my best friend. And you remind me of him, so much."

"We need to talk about Justin and Erin," Nikki said. Not her father who she barely remembered. Her mother had never recovered from his suicide. She'd sunk into a deep depression and eight years later died from pancreatic cancer. Nikki used to dwell on how different life might have been if her father had chosen to live. Now she never thought about him. Not much anyway.

"Well," Robert said, shaking his head. "We know Justin had nothing to do with Erin's disappearance. Your statement put him in the clear."

"What do you mean? My statement? Didn't other people see him in the arena?"

Robert shrugged, focusing on calling Gunner around to the side of the desk. Gunner, for his part, was happy to walk over and have his ears scratched. But it was obvious Robert was evading her question.

"Other people saw Justin that day, right?" she persisted. "Boarders? Barn workers? Someone besides me?"

"There's no sense digging this all up."

"But I'd like to know. I don't remember what I told the police."

"Of course you don't remember," Robert said. "You saw everything through the eyes of a traumatized twelve-year-old. Let's just leave it. But I find it surprising that they let Justin have the case yesterday...considering."

Nikki picked up a pen, rolling it between her fingers. Some of the events around Erin's disappearance were crystal clear, others blurry. She remembered accusing Justin, saying it was his fault because he'd let Erin skip barn work and go on the trail ride. And she'd forever regret that she'd lashed out like that, desperate for someone else to blame. He'd just nodded, full of compassion, understanding her guilt and willing to shoulder the blame. Then he'd hugged her and she felt him shaking, and it was clear he was just as affected.

Besides, he'd been in the arena the entire afternoon.

But who had he been teaching? She'd cancelled her lesson, needing the time to clean Erin's stalls. Someone had been riding though. She remembered the rhythmic thud of hooves and how the sound kept her company as she pushed the wheelbarrow up and down the aisle. Adding shavings to the stalls was usually tedious work but she'd been grateful to see the wheelbarrows had already been filled. She'd even had time to practice braiding Harry's mane, and it hadn't looked half bad.

Had she even looked in the arena? Or had she been too preoccupied wondering when the riders would return and hoping Erin was having a good time.

Justin certainly hadn't been coaching when she found him later that day. He'd been outside by the paddocks. She remembered how he'd leaped onto Diesel's bare back, guiding the big horse with only a rope and halter. The paddocks were close to the trees... And the trail.

She didn't like the direction her mind was spiraling and she twisted her chair to the right, to the left, then back again. But her dark thoughts wouldn't leave. She remained silent for a long minute. The only sounds were Gunner's satisfied groans as Robert scratched the base of his ears.

Finally she looked at Robert. "I'd like to read the barn interviews from that day. Is there any way you can arrange it?"

She knew she was asking a lot. Cold files were kept in secure storage. She didn't want to know the names of Robert's inside contacts. But he always seemed to know what was going on. And Robert had never disappointed her yet. Not only did he help drum up business but he was a gold mine of advice, and when necessary, inside information.

"I won't be able to get the actual file," Robert said, "now that my buddy has retired. But I could probably get pictures. Why don't you drop by for supper tonight and hopefully I'll have something. But aren't you and Justin friends? Are you sure you want to dredge this up?"

"Absolutely sure." She folded her arms across her chest, smothering the apprehension hidden behind her words.

CHAPTER TWELVE

NIKKI ALWAYS ENJOYED visiting Robert and his dog friendly property. He'd fenced a section of his yard, separating the swimming pool from the grassy section where Gunner was free to roam. The pool held many wonderful memories. It was the place where she and Erin had learned to swim, squealing in childish delight when Robert tugged them around on a bouncy float.

But today she was too apprehensive to step out and relax on the patio, despite the refreshing breeze that gusted through the screen door. Surely someone else had seen Justin that horrible afternoon when Erin had vanished. Worse, what did it mean if she'd been the only one to provide him with an alibi?

Her gaze shot to Robert's cell phone, her fingers clicking an impatient dance on the kitchen counter. "Has anything come in yet?" she asked.

"From what?"

"Your contact in cold cases."

Robert snapped open two cans of beer, poured them into chilled glasses then scooped up his phone and checked his messages.

"Not yet," he said, peering up from the screen. "But the shift hasn't changed yet. It takes time to pull the file and take the pictures. And he won't send everything. Just the interviews from the people at the barn."

Nikki nodded and rolled her shoulders, unable to remain still. She swung open the bottom cupboard, searching for Robert's wooden salad bowl, then realized it was already on the table. Turning, she pulled open the cutlery drawer, needing to keep her hands busy.

"The patio table's already set," Robert said, waving the barbecue tongs. "I just need to grill the steaks. Why are you so impatient anyway? There's nothing new."

She picked up her beer, pressing the cold glass against her cheek. Of course there was nothing new. But she was an adult now, with a different perspective, and the rare opportunity to read her interview—along with those of the other kids'—was all consuming. After seeing the stable again and re-acquainting herself with its labyrinth of trails, maybe she'd see something that would provide fresh insight. There was no question she totally trusted Justin. But it bothered her that she couldn't remember who else had been at the barn that day, other than the three girls who had gone with Erin on the trail ride. There had to be someone else who had confirmed his presence.

"I'm just eager to see the interviews from all the kids," she said. "Including me."

"And that's the information I requested." Robert's voice turned distracted as he dug into the freezer then triumphantly pulled out a meaty bone. "I'm going to take this out to Gunner," he said. "It's a special cut, organic kangaroo. The people at the store told me that dogs love them."

Some of her worry softened as she glanced out the wide French doors. Gunner sat outdoors on the patio, staring patiently through the screen, aware Robert never failed to bring him a bone. It was as much a ritual as her ice-cold beer.

"I'm surprised you didn't ever get a dog of your own," she said, once Robert slid the door shut and stepped back inside.

"I love dogs," Robert said. "But it wouldn't have been fair. Police work involves a lot of night shifts and overtime. When I left and started the detective agency, it was more of the same. Maybe if I had someone home to help, it would have been different."

"You think I'm not fair to Gunner?"

"Not at all. You always put his needs first. But I didn't want to have to hurry home. Or miss a golf tournament because I had a dog that needed a walk. How many activities have you turned down because you wanted to be with Gunner?"

Nikki gave a rueful tip of her glass. There was no doubt that Robert enjoyed an active social life. He was a competitive golfer and still very fit. The silver hair around his temples, instead of making him look older, gave him a distinguished look. She'd always hoped her mother would see him as more than a friend but that had never happened. She suspected it was because Robert had been her father's best friend, and they hadn't been able to move past that. Her mother had died six years ago and Robert had given the eulogy. Everyone in the church had cried.

She reached over and squeezed his hand. "You've always been so supportive. I don't know what we would have done without you."

"You'd have managed. You're the most capable woman I've ever met." But his eyes glistened even as a smile worked over his face. "And please don't ever give me a puppy."

She laughed. They'd had this conversation before, right after he'd added the fence for Gunner and she thought it would be great if he owned a dog too. But admittedly puppies were a lot of work and he didn't have a friend like Sonja. Her farm, along with its motley group of animals, had been a godsend for a lively Shepherd. Robert's pool deck was too pristine, the flower gardens a little too immaculate, and though he gamely tried to hide it, it was obvious he wasn't a fan of Gunner's heavy shedding.

He stepped outside to barbecue the steaks and she wandered into the living room, reassured that the pictures on the mantle remained unchanged. Robert was intensely loyal and not the type to sweep someone's life beneath the carpet. Her mother and sister smiled back at her, still occupying their place of honor. They looked so alike with their fair skin and blond hair. She refused to look at the square picture to the far left.

The patio door slid shut.

"It's not healthy to pretend he never existed," Robert said, walking up to stand beside her. "I've never had a braver friend. Paul was always there when I needed him."

Nikki's mouth tightened. "He wasn't a good father though," she said. "Or husband. Mom was never the same afterwards. She loved him so much."

"He was a handsome devil." Robert's sigh was long and low. "Some people have one love in their life, and he was hers."

Nikki turned and stared grudgingly at the framed photo, the one with Robert and her father, handsome in their uniforms, taken on the day they graduated from the police academy. She had the same coloring and she supposed they looked alike, although she would never admit it. Not even to Robert. She barely remembered her dad, only that her mother had always been happy when he was around and life had seemed full of love and laughter.

He'd shot himself a day before her fifth birthday. Her mother hadn't smiled much after that. And his death certainly hadn't helped Erin. She'd grown from a happy, confident girl into a moody teenager, who'd completely drained their mother of every ounce of energy.

A cell phone chimed, announcing an incoming text. Nikki swung around. Robert was already hurrying to the kitchen for his phone and she followed closely on his heels.

His brow furrowed as he read the text. "That's odd," he said, slowly placing his phone back down. "We can't get the information because Erin's case file has been signed out for the last few months."

"What does that mean?"

"The usual reason is that it's been reactivated." However, Robert's voice was troubled and it was obvious he was reluctant to say more.

"We know it hasn't been reactivated," she said. "So what are the unusual reasons?"

"My contact says the file might contain information that someone prefers remain unseen," Robert said. "And that they want to know the identity of anyone who shows an interest."

Nikki's calm tone masked her dread but her fingers clenched the counter. "Can your friend tell us who signed it out?"

"Yes." Robert gave a troubled nod. "Justin Decker."

CHAPTER THIRTEEN

THE STEAK ROBERT SERVED was delicious but Nikki's appetite had disappeared. She toyed with her food, barely noticing when Gunner picked up his bone and trotted off the patio and onto the pool deck. She should have opened the gate to the grassy section while Robert was barbecuing, but her mind had been whirling, trying to convince herself that there were plenty of good reasons why Justin would have removed Erin's file.

"You say Justin arranged for a cadaver dog?" Robert said. "If that was a few months ago, he probably just forgot to return the evidence files."

Nikki appreciated how Robert was trying to find excuses for Justin. However, she shook her head. "It wasn't recent though. That was years ago, when he first made detective. I guess something else re-kindled his interest." Unless he didn't want anyone to see the interviews. And no matter how hard she tried to banish that thought, the facts were troubling. Especially since Justin had claimed he hadn't looked at Erin's file in a while.

"I remember talking to Detective Beryl McClelland that day," Nikki said. "She took me in the riders' lounge and gave me a stick of spearmint gum. I assumed she was the one who interviewed the other girls. I actually called her the first week after I passed my exam."

The detective had been polite. Promised to let Nikki know if she had anything new and congratulated her on getting an investigator's license. But Nikki never heard from her and later learned McClelland had retired and moved to Queensland.

"I'd like to talk to Detective McClelland again," Nikki said. "If I can find out where she lives."

"Worth a try," Robert said. "I have a buddy in records who could be persuaded to give us her address. McClelland might have kept some private notes from that day. I know I did."

Nikki jerked forward so abruptly her fork clattered on the side of the plate. "You have information? But you were a cop, not a detective."

His face darkened and she realized she should have tempered her words. Robert was a bit sensitive about never making detective.

But he only gave a sad smile. "I wanted to find Erin as much as you did. I didn't think your mother could take another loss... Hey," he said, whipping his head around. "Better get your dog out of there."

She followed his gaze. Gunner was sitting by the manicured flowerbed, the kangaroo bone at his feet. He knew he wasn't allowed to dig there but soft dirt was tempting, especially when he had a bone.

"Over here, Gunner." She rose from the patio table and strode toward the side gate that opened onto the grass. "Bring it."

He scooped up his bone and trotted toward her, his tail wagging.

"This is better," she said, trailing her hand over his head. "Safer too."

She always worried he might fall in the pool and not be able to climb out. Accordingly Robert had separated his yard, even to the point of adding a special dog gazebo. He'd even offered to install pool steps at the shallow end but she didn't want Robert going to any more trouble. Besides, Gunner was content, already headed toward the shaded gazebo with the bone protruding from the sides of his mouth. No doubt, he'd try to bury it again. She'd have to keep a watchful eye. Digging was the big downside of Robert's bone generosity.

She trudged back to the patio and her cold dinner. Robert's appetite seemed similarly diminished as both of them had only picked at their steaks. Gunner was going to be one lucky dog.

"If you kept any personal notes about Erin's case," she said, folding her napkin and placing it beside her plate, "I'd love to see them."

Robert arched a surprised eyebrow. "But you already have them. And like I told you before, I never had anything official, just bits and pieces along with your mother's thoughts. They're in a green folder with Erin's name on it. The file should still be in your office. Check there tomorrow and if you can't find it, give me a call."

Nikki gathered their plates, wondering how she'd missed seeing Erin's name. She'd reviewed everything when she'd taken over Robert's business and moved into her own space. Most of his files had been sent to storage. But if there was anything in her office that could shed light on Erin's disappearance, she certainly wasn't going to wait until tomorrow.

Forty-five minutes later she was driving down the street in front of her office, searching for a parking spot. Usually she used the gravel lot behind the building. But at this time of night it was easy to snag a spot closer to the front door.

She eased her car alongside the curb and opened the back door. Gunner leaped onto the sidewalk. Street lights spotlighted a scatter of activity: a shopper clutching a bag from a late-closing shoe store, three teens leaning against a car with a pizza box spread on the hood, and a pair of whip-thin joggers who gave Gunner a cautious berth.

Gunner barely looked at the joggers, his attention focused on the teens and their pizza. He'd already enjoyed a meaty bone, the bulk of two steaks and a serving of kibble, but—much to her chagrin—had developed an insatiable craving for Italian food. Pepperoni pizza was his favorite.

"Come on, Gunner," she said, trying to hurry him into the building before the owner of the pizzeria spotted them. But it was too late. She caught the flash of a white apron and then Vinny's toothy smile. Seconds later, Vinny bustled through his doorway and onto the patio fronting the sidewalk.

"Are you hungry, Nikki?" he called. "I have your table ready. Please, come inside." He held the door open, waving his arm with a flourish more appropriate to a five-star restaurant.

"Not tonight, thanks Vinny," she said. "I already ate."

"A glass of wine then? And some leftovers for Gunner?"

Gunner greeted that offer with an enthusiastic tail wag then tilted his head, staring longingly through the window, aware that inside was unlimited pepperoni and a place where he was treated like a rock star.

Vinny hadn't always been so welcoming. When Nikki first leased the adjacent office, he'd complained that a big dog would scare away customers. His opinion had changed the night a strung-out addict had rushed into his restaurant, waving a gun and demanding the contents of his cash register.

Nikki and Sonja had been eating pizza on the outdoor patio with Gunner curled beneath the table. The takedown had been quick and explosive. Gunner had caught the man in three strides and the picture of a German Shepherd pinning the thief on the sidewalk—surrounded by fluttering dollar bills—had gone viral. People had stampeded to Vinny's, at first out of curiosity. But they'd returned because of the mouth-watering and inexpensive Italian food.

Somehow the rumor started that Gunner lived in the back of Vinny's restaurant. There hadn't been a robbery attempt since, and Vinny confided that he'd increased his menu, tripling his profits.

"Maybe you'll drop by for breakfast this week?" Vinny asked, dropping to one knee so he could thoroughly scratch Gunner's chest. "You and Sonja can be the first to try our new espresso machine. We're starting a breakfast menu. I promise our biscotti will always be crunchy and great for dipping."

"You're open for breakfast now!" Nikki reached out and gave him a celebratory fist bump. Vinny and his partner worked long hours, and it was gratifying to see their hard work rewarded.

"Yes," Vinny said. "So you won't have to go far for good coffee. You can pick it up here, on the house."

Nikki nodded but there was no way she'd accept free coffee every day. It was gratifying that Vinny was appreciative though. In the old location, Robert had been the respected investigator and she'd been the rookie. Now she was building her own connections, and it was all thanks to Gunner—the dog Justin had so generously given her.

She promised Vinny she'd drop by soon then headed toward her office building, her steps quickening as her thoughts swung back to Justin. Her feelings about him had never been simple. Now they were more complicated. But even if it turned out she'd been the only person to vouch for his presence that day, it was crazy to think he'd had anything to do with Erin's disappearance.

Justin had always been professional, squashing overtures from every fawning female, no matter the age. He certainly hadn't given Erin extra attention, at least, not that Nikki remembered. But would she have noticed? Back then, she'd been oblivious to anything but Stormy. And making sure she and Erin kept their jobs.

Certainly those last months, the way Erin dressed had changed. She'd also been acting weird. She had always been moody but on good days she liked to recite everything that happened in school. That had stopped. At the time Nikki had been relieved not to have to listen to her sister's endless drama. There'd been a few boys Erin had gushed about: a senior on the football team, her nerdy lab partner, and some tall guy who ate lunch with her whenever he and his girlfriend had a fight.

But as Nikki remembered telling the detective, she didn't know the boys' last names and didn't think her sister had seen any of them outside of school. Of course, at times Erin had been surprisingly secretive.

Sighing, Nikki followed Gunner down the hall to her office and pressed in the security code. The lock beeped at the same time as her cell. She pushed open the door, pulled out her phone and checked the screen. Her heart immediately kicked into overdrive.

It was Justin, and he wasn't calling from his office. It was from his personal cell and the significance of that left her gripping the phone even tighter.

She wasn't ready to talk to him yet, torn between the thrill of last night's heated embrace and prickly questions about his whereabouts the day Erin disappeared. It would be best to call him back after she found the file, after she'd reassured herself that he'd been in the arena the entire time.

She reminded herself that she trusted him. Totally. But it was the memory of his hot kiss that left her rushing to press the green button.

"Drake Investigative Services," she said, aiming for calm and professional. Instead, her words came out annoyingly breathy.

"Nikki."

Her name was all he spoke. But the sound of his deep voice made her insides do funny things. Clearly he was waiting her out, letting her set the tone. Detectives were good at that. But she'd taken similar training.

"Justin," she replied.

He chuckled, a rich and deep-throated sound that made her aching to see him, when and wherever he chose. At the office, at the park or in the back of his SUV. But his voice turned cop serious. "I wanted to let you know that Matthew Friedel made a full confession."

It was wise not to admit that Robert had already updated her. Police didn't like to think their office had leaks. And Justin played by the rules. It was typical he didn't reveal that Savannah was pregnant, ever respectful of the victim.

"I'm glad," she said simply. "You must be exhausted."

"Heading home now," Justin said. "But tomorrow I'm driving out to the K9 center to meet with the team that worked the case. Wonder if you'd like to join me?"

Yes! was her silent answer. But it was a two-hour drive there and back, possibly a full day's excursion, depending on Justin's business. Gunner would be okay at home and with his dog door, he could step out into the tiny yard whenever he needed. But maybe he'd be happier if she left him in her office and arranged for Sonja to take him for a noon walk. She tugged at her lower lip. Time management was a constant issue with pets.

"It's okay to bring Gunner," Justin said.

She blew out a relieved breath. It was always easier when her dog was invited too. But offers like this were often followed by the suggestion that it might be best to leave him home. That was one of the reasons she visited Sonja's farm so often, because her friend genuinely welcomed both her and her dog.

She waited for Justin's next words, guessing he would add that the center didn't normally allow outside dogs. And was totally understandable. She didn't want Gunner to go simply because Justin had enough rank to pull favors.

"Everyone there will be happy to see him," Justin said.

She smiled into the phone, knowing she could count on him to tell the truth. And that he understood Gunner's acceptance was important. "You're awesome," she said.

Justin's laugh was quick and entirely too sexy. "Hold that thought."

CHAPTER FOURTEEN

NIKKI SHOVED THE PHONE in her back pocket, her heart still pounding at the prospect of spending a full day with Justin. It had been years since they'd done that. Ever since Erin's disappearance he'd been in and out of her life, never staying long but always appearing at the best and worst possible times.

She'd never forget his chilling anger when she and a teenage friend had been caught hotwiring cars. Her friend would never forget it either; in fact, the guy had been so spooked he was now a counselor for troubled youth.

But Justin had a gentle side. He was the one who'd found her the last time she ran away from home to live on the streets. Nikki doubted her mother had even noticed her absence. Justin had though.

"You'll never find Erin like this," he had said, sitting down beside her and handing over a hot coffee and sandwich. He'd been a police officer then, but hadn't seemed concerned about the dirt staining his crisp uniform or that the other park denizens were shooting him looks bordering between wary and openly hostile.

She'd denied Erin was the reason of course, but after much argument, anger and protest, he'd helped her come up with a new plan: She would bide her time until she was older, until she'd gained the necessary skills and training, and was better equipped to hunt down the creep who had taken her sister.

"I don't want to be a cop like you though," she had said, busy stuffing the sandwich into her mouth. "Too many rules. I want to make someone pay for what they did. Better to be a freelancer or assassin, something like that."

"I don't want to have to arrest you," Justin had said gravely. "So why don't you finish high school and then decide."

He'd gone on to talk about the importance of studying hard, avoiding a criminal record and focusing on her goals, but it was only when he promised to take her to the shooting range that she'd agreed to return home. He also promised to teach her self-defense and those lessons had turned into the highlight of her week. She couldn't remember why or when they stopped.

It might have been because Robert had given her a part-time job in his new investigative office. Or that Justin had started bringing his girlfriends to the lessons and though the women tried hard to be nice, it was obvious she was a third wheel.

Admittedly she had abandonment issues. However, Gunner had helped a lot with that. She glanced at her dog who'd already flopped down on his mat, happy to be wherever she was. Dogs were loyal, much more than people—not counting Robert and Justin of course. At various points in her life, each of the two men had been her anchor. And she couldn't believe she'd allowed herself to have misgivings about Justin, enough that she'd neglected a steak dinner simply to speed over to her office and check some files.

She was here now though, and might as well see it through. She knew the contents of *her* file on Erin by heart, painstakingly gathered over the years. However, she'd never viewed Robert's personal notes. Didn't realize he had kept a separate folder.

She hurried across the room to the locked cabinet. Her filing system was low tech, the same one she'd inherited from Robert: current cases on the top shelf, office files and accounts receivable on the middle, and old cases crammed on the bottom. Robert had turned over all the paperwork for any jobs she'd been involved with. They occupied the bulk of the cabinet since her completed cases were stored on a secure central computer.

His system was bulky and space consuming, but she was always respectful of handwritten notes. They conveyed thoughts and intuition while typed reports were proper and precise, focusing on hard facts.

She slid her hand behind the framed picture of Erin, retrieved the hidden key, and unlocked the bottom drawer. It had been months since she'd opened it and the green folders were stuffed so tightly it was hard to read the labels.

She switched from kneeling to sitting cross-legged, resigned to starting at the far end and checking each file. Even then she almost missed the folder. Robert hadn't even properly labeled it, "E Drake" was all it said, as if it hurt him too much to write Erin's name. She understood the feeling.

Opening the folder, she spread it on her lap, too impatient to move to the comfort of her desk. She flipped through countless scraps of paper, coffee-stained notes, and even an ancient school record listing all of Erin's classmates. Robert may have thought his rough notes didn't contain any pertinent information but it was obvious he'd worked zealously on Erin's investigation, long after official interest had fizzled. Some of his pages had been torn from notebooks, tattered and barely legible. But he'd also documented numerous visits to Nikki's house.

At the time, she'd thought he was bringing companionship and groceries, trying to help her dysfunctional mother through a dark time. But now she remembered his persistent interest in Erin's friends: who they dated, how they acted and the types of cars they drove.

Robert's questions had been gentle though, unlike her mother's which had often turned accusatory: "Why did you encourage Erin to go on a trail ride with those girls? Why didn't you stay with her? Why didn't you care enough to know who she was dating?"

The questions usually resulted in her mother crumbling into apologetic tears, leaving Nikki feeling even more guilty. Most times, she'd fled to her room, crushed and wishing *she* had been the daughter who'd vanished that day.

She blinked back her welling emotion and flipped through the collection of papers, searching for the date of Erin's disappearance.

Robert had been a beat cop, never a detective, so he didn't have official access to the investigation. His only role had been canvassing the neighborhood, checking if home owners had spotted any unusual vehicles. But he'd conducted his own research, gathering facts and observations, ripping the paper from his notebooks and keeping them safeguarded. Most of this stuff she knew by heart. After she'd earned her PI license, she and Robert had spent months rehashing Erin's case. To no avail.

A familiar address caught her attention: 93 Quarry Road, the farmhouse across from the stable and still owned by Jed Carver. The farmer had often been working on his fencing when the school bus stopped at the bottom of the barn's long driveway. Erin and the older girls had ignored him, his existence meaningless, but Nikki remembered how Carver had always been eager to talk. Robert had circled Carver's address and then ticked it off, noting that the man had attended a farm auction that day.

She leaned back against the cabinet, staring at Carver's name. She remembered his alibi. The day after completing her PI program, his farm had been the first place she'd visited. He appeared to be a harmless old man, still struggling to keep his rotting fences upright. Like Robert, she'd checked him off her list of suspects. But maybe she should pay him another visit. Carver owned a large and secluded property. Gunner wasn't a cadaver dog but he was good at finding old dog bones. And he had great instincts.

Chilled by the idea of a body, she shoved the scrap of paper to the side and returned to flipping through the file. The couple who used to live at 29 Quarry Road had reported seeing a red sports car at four-thirty that day. The car had streaked past, almost clipping their mailbox. The woman was sure the car had come from the stable but the man suspected it was someone dumping off another unwanted pet. Police had never been able to identify the driver, despite numerous appeals to the public.

Had the car really come from the barn? If so, was it a boyfriend or boarder? Robert had included the same questions in the typed notes he'd handed over to Nikki. But the sports car had remained a dead end.

After Nikki obtained her license, she'd tracked down every worker, supplier and boarder at the barn, including the three girls who had abandoned Erin by the brook. They were still plagued by varying degrees of guilt. Two of them had bent backwards to help, impressed that Nikki was working in an investigative office. The third girl, Theresa, had tried to hire Nikki to follow her boyfriend on a stag weekend. But none of the three recalled a male friend with a sports car—or a boyfriend of any sort.

"Don't you remember?" Theresa had said. "Back then we were all crushing on Justin. He was like a gorgeous god and he wasn't that much older. And, to be honest, if he had ever paid us any attention, we would have been terrified."

Terrified. At the time, Nikki had thought it was an odd word. Theresa always had an affected way of talking that hadn't diminished with age. Besides, Justin could be terrifying when he was angry, especially if one didn't know him. But he'd always treated staff and boarders fairly; he'd even left snacks in the barn whenever they worked late.

She'd been surprised he remembered Erin's preference for banana muffins. Had never imagined he'd noticed. In fact, Erin had once complained that Justin was way nicer to Nikki than he was to her. Yet Robert seemed to think Erin and Justin had been close.

She squeezed the bridge of her nose, staring unseeingly at the file. She shouldn't let the fact that Justin remembered her sister's favorite muffins bother her but if she didn't recall that, it left her questioning the clarity of her other memories. Justin had wanted to fire Erin that day—she definitely remembered that.

Had it been for other reasons though and not because of Erin's laziness? Would the police have considered Justin a suspect if Nikki hadn't provided him with an alibi? Surely someone else had seen him in the arena.

She continued scanning the notes, trying not to be sidetracked. Robert had kept a list of names: nine girls and one eight-year-old boy named Jimmy, all present on the afternoon Erin had vanished. She had a more extensive version of this list. She and Robert had compiled an in-depth history of the families on the chance that an acquaintance of the boarders had driven to the barn and followed the girls into the woods.

Robert had drawn a heavy line through Jimmy's name. The eight-year-old had been picked up by his dad at four o'clock, immediately after his riding lesson. Jimmy's father had lingered to talk to Justin. Apparently he'd wanted his son to ride in the upcoming show but Justin insisted Jimmy needed more instruction.

Nikki allowed herself a little smile. She remembered Jimmy and his curly hair. At first, he'd been a pain in the ass, following her around, peppering her with questions. He'd only been there because his mother insisted he learn to ride. But Jimmy wasn't a bad kid and when Justin saw her helping, he'd let her ride Stormy in the arena during Jimmy's lessons, provided she stayed out of the way. Having another pony around helped keep Jimmy's mount calm, and the end result was that she received extra instruction.

At one time, Jimmy's father had been high on her suspect list. Jimmy had confided that his parents were separated and that his dad had a bunch of girlfriends, all "way younger than Mom." But after Jimmy's lesson that day, he and his father had driven directly to Disney World. It was unlikely Erin could have been in the trunk the entire time, and even more unlikely that Jimmy's father would have known how to properly tie her horse to a tree.

It was the horseman's knot that was most perplexing. When Justin arrived in the clearing, Pancho had been tied with a quick release knot, not something the average rapist would know. Of course, Justin knew how to tie a knot. He'd always stressed the importance of keeping a halter beneath the bridle so horses could be safely tied on a trail ride. Or in an emergency.

Nikki flipped faster through the notes, hating her thread of suspicion and desperate to find someone else who had seen Justin that fateful afternoon.

Robert had sketched a timeline, marking the approximate time the boarders had left Erin in the clearing to the time they'd returned from the trail ride. There had been five people in the barn between four and six o'clock. One girl had been cleaning tack, another braiding a mane—Nikki remembered comparing their braids—and one was playing a game on her phone. The other two had been setting up jumps in the outside arena. No one reported having a lesson after Jimmy's. But Robert had drawn a heavy line through Justin's name. *Not a suspect, presence in arena confirmed by Nikki.*

Oh, God. Her chest kicked and for a moment she stopped breathing. Had she been the only one to clear Justin? Surely one of the other five kids had seen him too.

She grabbed her phone and called Robert.

"You're at the office, aren't you." Robert gave a knowing chuckle. "I should have guessed you wouldn't be able to wait until morning. Did you find the file?"

"Yes, it was in the bottom drawer. I just have a quick question." She cleared her throat, trying to sound casual, as if his answer wasn't important. "Why did the detectives believe Erin left the clearing willingly?"

"Because she took good care of her horse," Robert said promptly. "The saddle was loosened and the horse was tied in the shade with some sort of horse knot. What's the name of that knot?"

"Quick release," Nikki said, her throat tightening. She took another quick swallow. "Did the police look closely at everyone at the barn? Everyone who knew how to tie a horse?"

"Certainly, but there were only five other girls. The owners were away and the boy's dad had a solid alibi. And of course you saw Justin riding."

She squeezed her eyes shut. So she *had* been the only one to provide him with an alibi. And Justin had been alone when he found Erin's horse. He'd told her to wait at the barn. She remembered how he'd burst from the woods, riding his horse and leading Pancho. Maybe Pancho hadn't actually been tied in the clearing. Maybe the horse had been tied somewhere else, closer to the secret trail or the staff parking lot, and the entire search had been misdirected.

"I see," she said, and her voice sounded far away, as if somebody else were talking, someone calm and controlled whose world wasn't suddenly spinning. "So either Erin tied Pancho," she said, "and walked away *or* else she was taken by someone who knew about horses."

"That's right," Robert said. "The detectives maintained she walked away, although that's not what your mother thought."

Nikki pressed her shoulders against the cold cabinet, needing its support. She couldn't remember her mother's thoughts. They'd been too upset to talk: both mired down with unhealthy amounts of anger and guilt.

"What did Mom think?" Nikki said.

"She thought Erin was taken by someone she knew," Robert said, his voice reluctant. "That she was secretly seeing someone at the barn."

Nikki felt breathless, as if she'd run up a huge flight of stairs. But she had to ask. "And who did Mom think was this secret boyfriend? The mystery guy who took her?"

"Look, your mother was in a bad place. I don't think her thoughts were always based on fact."

Nikki closed the file, letting Robert know by her silence that she needed an answer. "Who did Mom think he was?" she prodded.

"Justin Decker."

CHAPTER FIFTEEN

THE MORNING SUN WAS bright and optimistic, bathing the road in a golden glow. Even so, it was unsettling driving with the man who Nikki's mother suspected had been responsible for Erin's disappearance.

Her mother had often been wrong, Nikki reminded herself, cautiously studying Justin, relieved her sunglasses hid her expression. Gunner had no such reservations. When Justin had pulled up this morning, the dog had greeted him with joyful exuberance, clearly still holding him high on his most favorite person list.

Justin had knelt and scratched Gunner's belly, but his astute gaze had been locked on her face. "What's wrong?"

She should have known he'd pick up on her misgivings and his obvious concern made her mother's suspicions seem even more off base. "Nothing," she'd said, giving a dismissive hand wave. "I was just thinking about Erin last night. Didn't get much sleep."

He'd reached out and squeezed her shoulder, his touch inviting. If she'd looked up, she sensed he would have kissed her. And she hadn't liked that the thought was so appealing, not when Erin deserved to be top of her mind. So she'd brushed past him, distrusting her instincts and annoyed at the way he made her heart pound. Her businesslike manner had set the tone for the day.

Justin may have been anticipating a more amorous welcome but if so, he hid it well, seemingly unfazed by her reserve. His driving was as smooth as ever, his hands relaxed on the wheel. But on two occasions he reached forward and needlessly adjusted his dashboard computer, a tell that maybe his cool façade had a few cracks. She certainly had a few questions, ones he could quickly clear up.

She shifted in the seat, studying his face. "Savannah's case made me wonder if there were any other guys around the barn back when Erin disappeared. You know, older men with cars hoping to take advantage of impressionable teens."

"We cleared that list," he said. "There was a hay delivery at ten fifteen that morning. One male driver. And the farrier made an unscheduled stop to tap a shoe back on Sasha. Theresa's mother dropped off a pair of riding boots an hour before the school bus arrived and Jimmy's father picked him up at four o'clock. Other than two boarders riding in the morning, there were no other visitors."

His total recall of that day had never disturbed her before. In fact, she'd found it comforting that someone else had been as affected. But now her suspicions churned, and she had to wonder why he remembered the day so well. "Sounds like you just read the file," she said.

"It's on my desk, Nikki. And though I haven't looked at it in a while, it's not something I'm likely to forget."

So he wasn't trying to hide the fact that he had Erin's file. That had to be a good thing. And she'd already established that the three men he mentioned were far from the stable at five o'clock that afternoon. Reliable witnesses had substantiated their whereabouts. That meant Justin had been the only adult male on the grounds. Still, the question remained: Had *she* been a reliable witness?

"I don't remember that afternoon as well as you," she said, jamming her sunglasses higher on her nose. "Jog my memory. I was cleaning Erin's stalls. And you were...?"

"Schooling Diesel."

Two words, that's all he'd give her? She studied his face, concerned about his reticence. He wouldn't have schooled Diesel for over two hours. In fact, she couldn't remember him ever riding a horse longer than an hour. And she didn't have the patience to ask ten questions when one would do.

"Was I the only one who gave you an alibi that day?" she blurted out.

He blinked, his shock obvious, along with another emotion she rarely saw from him—hurt. "No," he said slowly. "Theresa and Kimberly were in and out of the arena several times. And Timmy adjusted some jumps for me."

"Timmy left at four o'clock. And the girls went on their trail ride shortly after that. Exactly where were you between four-thirty and five?"

"I rode and cooled out Diesel. Then I worked outside."

His tone was level but he was uncharacteristically evasive. "Did they ever ask you to take a polygraph?"

"Not then," he said. "I've taken a few since."

"I'm sure someone like you could beat it."

He looked at her then, his eyes flat as coins. "No doubt."

Behind her, Gunner whined and stuck his nose over the middle console, taking turns nudging their shoulders. But Nikki could only grip her hands on her lap as Justin's words wormed around her brain. He'd just admitted he had no other alibi. And he knew where the secret path was, he'd owned a car with a trunk and he knew how to tie a quick release knot.

Silence stretched and she pressed back against the seat, chilled to the core.

"If you think I had a role in Erin's disappearance," Justin said, his voice toneless, "you're rather rash bringing it up now, while we're alone. I hope you aren't this reckless when you're working."

"I'm not reckless. I have Gunner." But her dog was resting his muzzle on Justin's shoulder, demonstrating that his allegiance was rather suspect. "And I have my gun," she added.

"I don't think so," Justin said, his voice eerily flat. "Unless it's in your dog pack which is in the back. But I don't believe you brought your Glock, judging by the way you tossed your pack around. Which shows you don't believe I was involved...or else you just don't think I would ever hurt you."

She shifted, her skin clammy as perspiration pricked the back of her neck. He was correct; she hadn't brought her gun. She only packed when she was working. And she couldn't imagine that Justin would ever hurt her. Hurt anyone. She blew out an impatient sigh. "Look, can you just tell me who else saw you in the arena? So I can let this go."

"You saw me riding between four and five o'clock. That was enough for the police."

"But I don't remember if I actually saw you," she said. "That part is blank."

"Don't worry. You didn't say anything that was untrue. Don't beat yourself up over it, Nik."

Her mouth tightened at the brush-off. He seemed to be trying to comfort her, as he'd always done in the past. But maybe he was playing her. Even though she'd known him for a long time, he remained an enigma. And maybe she should be treading more carefully. But he'd always been the one person who understood her guilt, along with her visceral need to find out what had happened to Erin. And she had to follow the evidence.

"Did you like Erin?" she pushed on, remembering her sister's tight breeches and how Erin had always brushed out her blond hair before stepping off the bus.

"I liked her as much as I liked any of the other kids," Justin said. "I didn't like that you always had to do her work."

Nikki shook her head. That wasn't what she meant at all. He was deliberately grouping Erin with a bunch of kids. Her mother had suspected Erin was having sex and frustrated that Nikki hadn't been able to shed any light on possible boyfriends. In a way, Nikki had been her sister's keeper. But in that department she'd failed miserably. And she wasn't going to let Justin evade her real question.

"What I really meant to ask," she said, "is did you ever screw her?"

He recoiled so sharply it pushed Gunner's head off Justin's shoulder. "Good God, Nikki."

The disgust in his voice couldn't be faked. But she wasn't going to stop. Investigative questions had a rhythm and she was just getting into it. "Mom thought Erin had a boyfriend. She blamed me for not being able to give her any names. You were around the barn. You owned a car."

"You think I seduced an underage girl?" He lifted his fingers off the wheel then tightened them again, his knuckles whitening. "You think I killed your sister and stuffed her in my trunk? Maybe strangled her and dumped her in the quarry? You really believe that?"

No, she didn't believe that. Not one bit. But her throat tightened at his bald words and the images they created and for a moment she didn't trust herself to speak.

She turned her head, hiding her emotion, blinking out the side window as his powerful vehicle sliced past a blur of trees. California was a great state for murder, with plenty of lonely spots for victims to disappear. Maybe there was even a deserted quarry beyond the ridge. Obviously the Savannah case had left her fragile, opening up old wounds, but part of her envied that family for having a body to bury.

Erin would have been twenty-eight this year. She might have been a mother now, making Nikki an aunt and Robert a pseudo-grandfather. And she finally accepted the bleak possibility that Erin was dead and her body would never be found.

"You're going to have to decide if you trust me," Justin snapped, misreading her silence. "By the way, do you have any other men on your suspect list? Because you better not question them when you're alone like this. You might not make it out alive."

"Sometimes I don't even care," she said, despair clogging her words.

He abruptly swung the wheel, bumping onto the shoulder of the road. The vehicle spun over the gravel, rocks pelting its underside. Gunner lurched forward, restrained only by Justin's strong arm. The SUV came to a shuddering stop.

He cursed. Then his hands were on her shoulders, his eyes drilling into hers. "Don't talk like that. Ever." He gave her a little shake. "You had a raw deal and lost your entire family. But you're brave, tough and resilient. I shouldn't have let you near that search. It stirred everything up."

His fingers felt like a vise over her shoulders and her hands shot for his wrists. If he were an average guy, she could break his hold. But Justin was no average guy and was also skilled at self-defense. They'd compared moves when she'd completed her black belt training. He'd blocked her every time.

She stared into his glittering eyes, seeing an emotion she'd never seen before. Not aggression or anger, but fear. And then she understood. *He was afraid she'd hurt herself.*

"You shouldn't be working alone as an investigator," he continued, his voice ragged. "Robert wasn't thinking straight, letting you take over a one-man business. It's too dangerous. Especially for an attractive woman like you."

"I'm not helpless," she said. "I could probably break your wrists in seconds." Probably not, but Robert had taught her the importance of a good bluff.

Justin snorted, the derisive sound loud in the confines of the car. "A trained man could overpower you. And that dog is no help at all." He shot a disgusted look at Gunner who was thumping his tail as if this was an interesting new game that he'd be delighted to join.

"That's not fair," she said. "Gunner knows you. If something happened to me, you're the person I'd want to have him."

"Nikki, please." He squeezed her shoulders even tighter. "Don't let this knock you down. You have to take care of yourself."

She was close enough to feel his pounding heart and his breath was more ragged than when they'd been running through the woods with Gunner. And the last of her despair eased away. She may have lost her beloved sister and both of her parents, but she still had someone who really cared. And for now, she didn't want to ask any more questions. Didn't need to.

She also didn't want him to worry needlessly.

"You misunderstood," she said. "My words didn't come out the right way. I'm not like my father. You don't have to worry about me."

He lowered his arms, straightened, and purposely wrapped his hands back around the wheel. But when he spoke, his voice was resigned. "Not sure if I can stop."

CHAPTER SIXTEEN

THE K-9 TRAINING COMPLEX was a sprawling property surrounded by a six-foot chain link fence. A rectangular building with attached dog runs sat next to a football-sized field sprinkled with agility courses. Nikki spotted at least three obstacles that involved ladders.

"Is that where Gunner flunked out?" she asked.

"Don't know," Justin said, his voice brusque as he expertly backed into a parking space beside several unmarked cars. He'd barely spoken since pulling over on the road earlier. However, she felt better after clearing the air. Based on his shocked reaction, she was positive he'd never had sex with Erin and even more certain he'd had nothing to do with her disappearance. His concern had been about Nikki's mental state rather than his own alibi.

Obviously he'd been hurt by her questions and that bothered her. She'd let the contents of an old file push her to hasty conclusions. She wished he had remained parked on the side of the road longer, but they'd both been processing each other's comments. It was clear he worried about her emotional health but she wasn't certain if that concern was related to her as a woman he wanted to date, or as the kid he'd always watched out for.

"We'll start outside," Justin said, turning off the ignition. "I'll let Tony know we're here."

Nodding, she pushed open her door, gathered Gunner's ball from her pack and clipped on his lead. He rose but remained rooted. A flurry of barks sounded from the outer kennels but Gunner stayed motionless as a statue.

"Let's go, boy," she said.

He stepped to the ground. But instead of an agile leap he moved stiffly, lacking his usual exuberance. She glanced across the hood of the vehicle at Justin, but he was talking on the phone, his back to her.

"What's wrong?" she asked, crouching beside Gunner. "Thirsty? Want some water?"

He didn't lift his paw or wag his tail, his usual response to any of her questions. He only pressed against her knee. Then she noticed something even stranger; he was trembling. He'd lived here before. Did he think she was bringing him back? Leaving him?

"Silly." She wrapped her arms around his neck and kissed his head. "I'm not dumping you. I love you."

Justin whirled, his hot gaze on her. Then his eyes shuttered. "Come on," he said as he jammed the phone in his pocket. "Tony will meet us at the second field."

She rose and walked beside him, still concerned about her dog. Gunner had stopped shaking but lacked any animation. He wasn't dragging on the leash but he acted like an aged family dog taking a duty walk rather than an energetic young Shepherd.

But as they passed a silver-colored horse trailer his head shot up, his ears pricking. Now he looked more like his normal self. And it hadn't been the other dogs that cheered him up, but the smell of horses.

"Do they keep police horses here?"

"No," Justin said. "But they periodically bring them in so the K-9s can get used to them. Sometimes it works the other way and the horses need exposure to dogs."

The stock trailer still carried the distinctive smell of hay and manure. Its presence explained why Gunner was so comfortable around animals. She'd assumed his breeding had left him with an affinity for livestock. But it had also been included in his training.

"They seem to think of everything," she said, "in order to turn out good K-9 teams."

"Yes, but sometimes a handler doesn't match up, no matter the pairing. Officers can flunk out too, just like the dogs. Some people just aren't good with animals."

"How do you know so much about this place?" she asked, racking her brain. Justin had been promoted from cop to detective. She didn't remember him ever working on a K-9 unit.

"Sometimes I have a young horse that needs more exposure," Justin said, his voice somewhat friendlier than it had been when he first parked. "They let me bring them here."

"So you still have your racehorse?" She smiled up at him, relieved to return to their earlier footing. "I remember going with you and your friend when I was in high school. It was a lot of fun."

But it had actually been bittersweet, the first and last time she'd been around horses since Erin's disappearance. When she'd returned home, pumped from the outing, her mom had freaked. "I can't believe you're so happy. Don't you feel guilty seeing those horses? Knowing they're the reason Erin's gone?"

Her mother had just been diagnosed with pancreatic cancer and Nikki's guilt had mushroomed. She'd dropped all extra activities and spent every minute of her spare time helping in Robert's new PI office, determined to focus on finding her sister. And Justin stopped inviting her to the races.

"The horse you saw race that day is long retired," Justin said. "She had three nice foals. I've owned quite a few Thoroughbreds since her."

"I never realized."

"You had a lot on your shoulders, Nikki. And not much support."

Except for Justin. He'd always tried to help. While Robert had been focused on her mother during her illness, Justin had been Nikki's rock. Her boyfriends had called him "that scary dude," and she'd often resented his all-seeing presence. But when she'd returned from her six-month sojourn to Japan, broke and homesick, Justin had been the one waiting at the airport.

He'd listened while she talked about her time in Japan and how much she had missed home, including the fast food. He'd immediately detoured to McDonald's and suggested she drop by the gym and show him and his girlfriend all her new moves. Minutes later, he'd been called out to a murder scene. He hadn't even had time to finish his burger. That's when she realized he was no longer a street cop. And that she really wasn't keen to meet any more of his girlfriends.

But he didn't appear to have a girlfriend now. She squeezed Gunner's leash, wondering what it would be like to have Justin all to herself, to be with someone whose company she actually enjoyed. Maybe this was a momentous day, a chance to clear the air about Erin and have a new beginning. A new type of relationship.

A door swung open. Tony stepped out, accompanied by a slight dark-haired woman who looked vaguely familiar. Probably not a dog handler; her heeled boots weren't made for running. She hurried toward them with a smile on her face, as if confident of her welcome.

"Fancy meeting you here," she said to Justin. Still smiling, she turned to Nikki. "Remember me?" she said. "I'm Lara. And I'd shake your hand but I've learned to be super careful around K-9s. Wow, you've grown up," she went on, giving Nikki an approving once-over. "Now I see why Tony was in such a hurry to get outside."

Lara. Then Nikki remembered. Lara was the woman who had gone to the track with them, back on that memorable day of horse racing. She was part of the mounted police unit and had taught Nikki how to bet. Obviously she was still involved with horses. She and Justin were already discussing one of the geldings she'd trailered in. Apparently the horse had been bitten on his hind leg and was wary of dogs, leaving him a liability on the street.

"Let's go to the agility field," Tony said to Nikki, "while those two talk about their hay burners. And for the record, I was not in a hurry to see you. I always rush my coffee." He gave a rueful swipe at the brown specks scattered over the front of his shirt.

"Hardly noticeable," Nikki murmured. She glanced at Justin but he was deep in conversation with Lara. Seconds later, they turned and headed toward the building. Neither of them looked back.

"Justin is picking up a K-9 report and Lara's horses are inside," Tony said, following her gaze. "We'll catch up with them later."

He guided her to a grassy field where he pointed out a variety of obstacles. Some of them looked fun, like the chain link fence and narrow teeter-totter. All appeared demanding. And a couple of them seemed impossible for any four-legged animal.

"That's so steep," she said, peering up at an angled ladder and attached catwalk. "Hard to believe any dog can do that."

"The Malinois don't have much trouble," Tony said. "They're the most agile. On the street if a unit runs into a high fence, it's easier for the handler to boost them over. A dog like Gunner is thirty pounds heavier." Tony's voice trailed off, his eyes narrowing on Gunner who was pressed against Nikki's thigh, looking everywhere but at the ladder. He was also shivering, even more noticeably than when he'd first stepped from the car.

"I don't know why he's upset," Nikki said, stroking his head in reassurance. "He was trembling in the parking lot too. At first I thought it was the other dogs or that he thought I was leaving him here. But now I think it's the obstacles."

"Then let's go inside," Tony said, pivoting away from the catwalk. "We have training rooms set up with everything from blood to drug caches. I bet he'll like searching more than he does the agility course."

But Nikki's investigative senses were tingling. Tony's voice was a little too jovial and for the first time since she'd met him, he wouldn't meet her gaze. "What aren't you telling me? What happened to him here?"

"I didn't want to upset you." Tony grimaced, finally looking her in the eye. "But you probably should know. I checked Gunner's records yesterday. He doesn't have a hind end problem. That's the good news."

"And the bad?"

"He had the misfortune to be teamed with an absolute idiot. The officer was determined to make the K-9 unit, at any cost. The first couple dogs he was matched with were disasters. He couldn't get them around the obstacle course, even after months of training. The dogs either refused or ran away. Gunner was his last chance. The guy was caught sticking him with a cattle prod, forcing him to climb. No doubt that's why Gunner is aggressive with men and the reason he'll never scale a ladder. Poor guy thinks he'll be electrocuted as soon as his paws touch the rungs."

"Let's get him inside." Nikki wheeled, keeping her voice calm for Gunner's sake. He was already upset and it wouldn't help for him to hear her anguish.

They strode in silence toward the building, Gunner's trembling fading, his head lifting with every step. But her steps were heavy knowing what he'd endured out in that field and she resolved that he'd never have to look at another damn ladder again.

"Does Justin know?" she asked, breaking the silence.

"No, and I'd prefer you didn't tell him. He's such an animal lover he'd probably make the officer disappear. The guy's career is already in the shitter."

"Rightfully so." Nikki spoke through tight lips then stilled, absorbing his words. Of course, Tony hadn't meant Justin would actually make the man disappear and she shouldn't take the statement so literally. Though she wouldn't mind if Justin exacted some sort of revenge on Gunner's abuser. But already her mind was drawing parallels and she had to remind herself that Erin had never hurt an animal. She'd loved the horses.

Neglecting to top the water buckets or to add more shavings had annoyed Justin but it wasn't abuse. Of course, there had been that time Erin lost her temper, yanking too hard on the reins and cutting her horse's mouth. And she could be overly aggressive with her spurs, especially if she'd been in one of her foul moods. If Erin hadn't been able to keep up with the boarders, would she have taken her frustration out on Pancho? Maybe bloodied his sides?

Was there a possibility she had been alive when Justin found her in the clearing but it was him who'd lost his temper? Was that why he refused to account for his missing half hour?

Nikki gave her head a disbelieving shake. Not possible. No way. Yet as she followed Tony toward the building, she couldn't prevent an insidious doubt from worming through her head.

Tony opened the door and stepped back, his eyes narrowing on her face. "What are you thinking?" he asked.

"Nothing good," she said.

CHAPTER SEVENTEEN

THE MAIN BUILDING WAS a hub of activity, punctuated with exciting barking and a staccato of human commands. Wailing sirens and flashing lights gave it a surreal appearance.

"That's the drug house," Tony explained. "We change the layout depending on the exercise. Detection training for narcotics and explosives starts there, then moves to more challenging sites. The siren gets the K-9s used to the real world."

Nikki stared in fascination at the organized chaos. A yellow Lab sniffed at the base of a patio table, a German Shepherd scratched furiously at a simulated office door, and a nimble Malinois balanced over a seesaw before disappearing into a blue tunnel. Only twenty feet away, a man with a bite sleeve skulked menacingly. Seconds later, a black-faced Shepherd launched through the air and grabbed his arm. Someone barked an order and the dog instantly released its hold.

No one paid any attention to her and Gunner: not the dogs or their handlers or the woman who was jotting notes on a huge whiteboard. It was reassuring that Gunner was no longer shaking, seemingly unfazed by anything inside the building. And now that her dog was relaxed—and she'd blocked out the ridiculous suspicions about Justin—she could concentrate on the exercises and gain a deeper understanding of Gunner's training.

"What's past the far door?" she asked, raising her voice so Tony could hear her over the din. "The one with the skull."

"Cadaver training," Tony said. "For dogs specializing in body searches. The smell in there can be overwhelming. We have everything from teeth, rotting tissue, even placentas." He jabbed a thumb over his shoulder. "Behind us is the entrance to the vet lab and rehab center. And through that green door is the quiet area where we start the younger dogs. Right now Lara has the space booked for a couple police horses. Let's start in there and come back when the sirens are off."

Nikki followed Tony into a quiet arena with reinforced walls and a deep woodchip floor. Justin stood next to a bearded man in khakis and held a thick-necked black horse. Dried sweat marked the horse's back in the shape of a saddle. The gelding was haltered now, looking half asleep, one of his hind legs tilted in rest. Lara was riding the second horse, a blaze-faced chestnut that she guided in circles around a parked cargo van.

"Earlier this morning," Tony said, his voice low, "that black horse was leaping around, totally petrified. He would have been a disaster on the street. Now we could put a barking dog on his back and he wouldn't care. I doubt he'll have to come back for more training. Lara is amazing."

Nikki gave a wistful nod. She'd shelved her love for horses but at one time they'd been the center of her existence. Both these animals were tall and kind-eyed and would no doubt be effective with crowd control, as well as street ambassadors. Obviously though, it wouldn't be safe having a twelve-hundred-pound horse that was skittish around dogs. How fortunate Lara could bring them here for exposure to K-9s.

She couldn't understand why Lara was circling the empty van though. Other than Gunner, there wasn't a dog in sight.

The man next to Justin gave a low command. A black and tan Doberman lunged inside the van, so unexpected it made Nikki jump. The Doberman jammed his jaws through the open window, barking furiously. The chestnut barely flinched. He swished his tail, indicating his displeasure, but continued his steady circling of the van.

Lara patted the horse's neck and nodded at the dog handler.

The man waved his hand. The Doberman leaped through the window and followed the horse, his nose close to the chestnut's thick tail. The handler said something, and the Doberman began barking again, all the while aggressively circling the horse. At one point, he even darted beneath the chestnut's belly. Other than flattening his ears, the horse remained impervious.

"This is a good test for both horse and dog," Tony explained. "The Doberman is good for this exercise because he doesn't care about horses, one way or the other. Some of the K-9s really like the animals so they're not as frightening. Horses can sense that."

Nikki glanced down at Gunner. He was the type of dog that horses liked. They seemed to know he bore no malice, his aggression reserved for strange men. And now that she knew about his abusive handler, she totally understood the reason.

Minutes later, Lara dismounted and gave her horse another approving pat. She was still smiling. So was Justin. In fact, they seemed to be sharing a private grin fest. Of course, they had much in common: law enforcement, dogs, horses. And likely Lara hadn't grilled him with questions more suitable to a suspect than an esteemed detective. That tended to dampen any relationship.

"I'm finished here, Tony," Lara called. "Thanks for letting me come by."

"Any time," Tony said. "Where's your partner?"

"Called in to court to testify. Luckily Justin was around. I don't believe your officers are comfortable with animals any bigger than a dog. Wish I had a good horseperson to follow the trailer and help unload." Lara's voice was light, but the invitation she shot Justin was unmistakable. Something twisted in Nikki's chest.

"Maybe Justin can help," Tony said. "I don't mind driving Nikki home. We've barely started the tour and there's a lot to see." He arched an eyebrow at Nikki. "I imagine you and Gunner want to stay and take part in some of the exercises? We also have a swimming pool he might like."

The chance to learn more about her cherished dog was tempting. But Nikki had no idea what Justin wanted. When he'd picked her up this morning, she'd thought, and hoped, it would be their first real date. And only a few short days ago, he hadn't seemed to want her socializing with Tony.

She shifted away, trying to catch Justin's eye. "I'm ready to go whenever you want," she said.

"No, that's fine." Justin shrugged as if happy with the new arrangements. And maybe Lara genuinely needed help. He wasn't the sort to desert a friend in need and he'd be the perfect assistant. He looked completely competent standing beside the huge horse—and so mouth-wateringly masculine—just as he'd looked at the stable when his good looks had put all the young girls in a tizzy.

Not her though. She hadn't cared about appearances. She'd liked Justin because he was always fair and respectful, with animals and people. And he'd been justified in wanting to fire Erin. Those last months she'd been doing eighty percent of her sister's work, on top of her own. Naturally he'd noticed.

He'd even commented that Erin was becoming a little short-tempered. Thankfully he'd never seen the aggressive way she used her spurs. *Or had he?* There hadn't been anything in Robert's file about spur marks on Pancho but would the police have checked the animal? Would they even have known to look?

"So, it's settled?" Tony asked, looking at Justin. "You'll go with Lara and I'll look after Nikki?"

Justin's head slanted, his amused gaze holding Nikki's. It was almost like old times when he knew she'd protest if anyone thought she needed looking after. Clearly he still thought of her as that stubborn, independent kid.

Admittedly her stubbornness remained; she still wanted to know what he'd been doing during that missing half hour. Of course the time gap wasn't related to Erin—it couldn't be—but it bothered her that he wouldn't account for his time. And the sheer polarity of her thoughts left her frowning.

Justin's mouth flattened and he gave another one-shouldered shrug as if happy to be rid of her. His gaze moved from her to Gunner. "Probably best not to ask him to climb any ladders while you're here. They seem to upset him."

His voice hardened. "Guess it's impossible to get rid of old baggage. No sense pushing."

She knew he was no longer talking about her dog. However, she gave an agreeable nod, hiding her dismay about being pawned off on Tony. Gunner was more honest, whining and waving a paw as if trying to convince Justin to stay. But the space was too great, Justin's expression too stony, and the distance between them seemed to stretch like an impossible chasm.

CHAPTER EIGHTEEN

"THANKS FOR DRIVING me home," Nikki said, as Tony slowed his vehicle in front of her house. "And for showing me the K-9 center. It's an amazing spot."

She'd learned a lot at the facility and would be a better partner to Gunner because of it. He'd participated in several exercises and she'd been so proud of him, especially when he was the second fastest dog to find the buried drugs.

"Gunner is definitely versatile." Tony pressed the stop button, turning off the car engine, apparently in no hurry to leave. His hand dangled over the gear shift, inches from her knee. "It was a good chance for you to meet some of the other teams. That could help down the road, especially since they can be a bit defensive of their turf. Speaking of that, what's the deal with you and Justin?"

Nikki felt her face flush. Robert had asked that same question before and she'd never known how to answer. She used to think of Justin as a solid friend but over the last few years something had changed, at least from her end. And after his passionate kiss, that shift had been seismic.

Now she couldn't look at Justin, or even think of him, without her insides melting with want. In an ideal world, he would have been the man sitting behind the wheel tonight. He would have addressed all her concerns about Erin, reassuring her of his whereabouts that day and his commitment to finding the truth. And then she would take his hand and lead him inside and probably they wouldn't even make it to her bedroom...

She realized Tony was watching, waiting for her to speak. But her feelings about Justin left her frustrated. And sad.

"My relationship with Justin isn't really any of your business," she said, crossing her arms.

"I'd like to make it my business." Tony flashed a mischievous smile, but his gaze was steady and it was clear he wanted an answer.

"I've known Justin since I was eleven," she said blowing out a resigned sigh. "He helped me through some tough times and is the reason I'm not locked up in prison somewhere. I think the world of him. But he's always been the one to set our boundaries so if you want anything more than that, you'll have to ask him."

Tony chuckled, a warm understanding sound that filled the car. "Justin is the guy who asks the questions. He doesn't like to answer them."

She gave a strained smile, remembering his evasiveness when she asked where he was that ill-fated afternoon at the stable.

Tony brushed her knee, a touch so quick and feather light it was hard to object. "I understand you and Justin got tangled up during your sister's tragedy and became good friends. It's habit for him to protect you, and vice versa. But I've also seen the way you look at each other. I'm just hoping the relationship doesn't extend to your social life."

"Wait." She jerked forward. "Justin told you? About my sister? About Erin?"

"Of course he didn't. He's tighter than a drum. I checked your background the same day I met you." Tony's chuckle was totally unrepentant. "That's what cops do when they meet someone who interests them. In my defense, it was completely justifiable since I was vetting you for our contract list."

His candidness was refreshing but somehow she doubted Justin would ever check police files on civilians. He was too correct, too respectful. On the other hand, it made things easier with Tony since now she wouldn't ever have to talk about Erin, a subject that generally invoked sympathy and dismay, along with morbid curiosity. There was nothing fun in Nikki's family history. Nothing except pain and loss.

"Your dad was a helluva cop," Tony said.

Her mouth gaped. That was the last thing she expected to hear and it took a full moment for her to recover. "Clearly you didn't go into my file deep enough," she snapped. "He shot himself when I was four. Left my mother and older sister devastated." And his decision had sent her family into a dark and downward spiral.

Behind her, Gunner whined, trying to press his nose against her neck. But Tony's car was equipped with a mesh screen that kept dogs in the back, and she accepted it wasn't just the conversation that bothered her but also the fact that she couldn't touch her dog. Having Gunner beside her helped her cope.

She reached for the door handle, needing to escape.

"Just a moment." Tony pressed a button on his dashboard and the screen smoothly lowered.

"The mesh is for my dogs' protection," Tony said. "I should have lowered it when we parked. I like to be able to reach my guys too."

His empathy was unexpected, especially after his ill-informed comment about her father. She gripped Gunner's neck, her fingers twining around his thick hair. Robert thought she needed to see her father with clearer eyes but he was wrong. Besides, her dad was dead—her mother and sister gone—so it didn't matter. Talking about him was pointless.

But Tony seemed determined to knock down her walls with one giant blow. He already knew everything about her yet he was still sitting in the car, discussing her life as if she were a normal person. He didn't seem at all worried about hitting minefields. He even recognized her attachment to a large, sometimes aggressive dog.

She turned away from Gunner, slowly dropping her arms. Small talk wasn't her forte and she'd always had a tough time knowing when guys were hitting on her or just being friendly. But at least Tony was open, a man who said what was on his mind and didn't have a secret agenda.

He chatted about the best pet foods, how air scent dogs could be trained to detect a virus, and why London on The Littlest Hobo was more famous than Rin Tin Tin. It was all rather interesting and she slowly relaxed, even to the point of tilting her seat so she could talk and pat Gunner at the same time.

Unlike Justin's car, there was no police terminal on the dashboard, no steel gun box or intrusive radio chatter. Dog beds took up most of the back, interspersed with bowls and water jugs. Clearly this wasn't a work vehicle but Tony's private car that he'd equipped with a mesh screen.

Then she understood. He had dogs. Not K-9s but pets. That's why he knew how helpful animals were when helping humans deal with stress. A smile split her face. "How many dogs do you own?" she asked.

"Five." Tony spoke rather sheepishly. "My Shepherd is three legged, the Lab is deaf and the other three are in various stages of retirement. But they were all police dogs and deserve a good home. They like to drive around with me. It makes them feel like they're still working."

"That is so sweet."

"Yes," he said. "It's my best pick-up line."

She laughed but knew there was a lot more to this man than his good looks and flirtatious comments. Best of all, he didn't seem insulted or prone to sulk that she didn't reciprocate his dating interest.

"I think it's fantastic." She was still smiling when she reached for the door handle. "Thanks for the educational day. You're very kind."

"Stubborn too. So I'm not letting Justin run me off. And if you just want to talk, I'm your man. Don't forget that I can pull a lot more interesting stuff from our police files. Did you know your dad worked undercover at the track? That he helped take down a major drug ring?"

"I'm not interested in talking about my father." In spite of Nikki's denial, her hand lowered from the door and she sank back against the seat. Her father had grown up on a farm and apparently loved animals. But her mother had deep-rooted allergies and they'd never been allowed to have any sort of pet, not even a guinea pig.

Robert had installed a washer and dryer by their back door so she and Erin could clean their clothes the moment they returned from the barn. It was surprising they'd even been allowed to work at the stable since their mother had always been red-eyed and sneezing after picking them up, and the effects had lingered for hours.

"Mom must have known a little bit about Dad's work," she said slowly. "She always had a love-hate relationship with horses. She let Erin and I work at a stable, but she was quick to blame them for Erin's disappearance."

"Laying blame is a normal coping mechanism."

She gave a reluctant nod. "Mom didn't have it so easy after Dad died. She adored my father. Not sure why."

Tony's chuckle was so quick and infectious even Nikki smiled. "Guess it's obvious I resent him," she said. "For leaving Mom and Erin."

"And for leaving you."

"Yes," she admitted.

CHAPTER NINETEEN

NIKKI LEANED BACK IN her office chair, clicking the tip of her pen and staring at her blank computer screen. She refused to type in her father's name. Didn't want to see the devastated faces, the funeral pictures or any clips of her sobbing mother. Her father was wrapped in the crux of the family's pain and loss, and she'd learned to control her bouts of nostalgia and what-ifs.

But Tony's comment last night left her curious. The racetrack sting had been an infamous case and one that had been touched upon in Nikki's investigative program. Maybe her father had done a special thing, something she should know about. Robert had tried talking about her father's police career but her mother had always shut him down, either breaking into tears or turning to stony silence. Nikki remembered Erin's solemn whispers that talking about *him* only made her mother sad. So her father had turned into he who must not be named, like a real-life Voldemort.

All Nikki could remember was a man who flung her in the air and called her tiger. He'd had a red beard that tickled her face and he always had time to push her on the swing. Everyone was happy when he was around. But after his suicide, her mother's tinkling laughter had turned into the rarest of sounds, and her subsequent death proved it was possible to die of a broken heart. Why had she loved him so much?

Nikki tossed the pen aside and typed in her father's name, along with the track. A score of articles popped up but nothing she didn't already know: Undercover agents had used racehorses to get close to a reclusive owner named Thomas Carlton. Their infiltration had resulted in convictions ranging from drug trafficking and money laundering to blackmail and murder. Some of the articles focused on Thomas Carlton's ruthlessness while unconfirmed sources gave lurid details about his now-divorced wife and their luxurious private life. But nothing was said about the officers involved. Naturally their identity had been protected. Crime bosses weren't the most forgiving of people.

She froze then checked the date. Eight years after Carlton had been sent to prison, Erin had disappeared. That was a huge time gap. *Still... Could they somehow be related?* She grabbed her phone and called Robert, her questions garbled and breathless.

He waited for her to finish then spoke with the patient tone that always calmed her. "So you're wondering if Carlton ordered Erin killed because he couldn't get back at your deceased father? Almost a decade later? Even though Carlton's locked up for life?"

It did sound far-fetched. Someone in the background suggested a three iron. She heard Robert say he needed a moment. Then he was speaking in the phone again. "I don't think so," he said. "Certainly the detectives didn't think there was any tie to Erin. It feels like a stretch."

She could feel him thinking though, weighing the possibility. Robert sometimes moved too slowly for her liking but he was thorough and methodical and never dismissed any of her ideas outright. Unlike the police.

She pressed on. "What exactly was Dad's involvement with the case? Would Carlton know him?"

"Absolutely. Your father was the reason they had enough evidence to go to trial."

"So he knew Dad." She waited, knowing from experience it was best to let Robert come to his own conclusions.

"Yes," Robert said. "Your dad posed as a horse groom and rescued Carlton from a mugging one night when the man was visiting the barn." Robert's voice was picking up steam now and it sounded like he'd moved away from his caddy. "Of course, the mugging was staged but Carlton was so impressed with his courage that he was hired as one of Carlton's drivers. Your mother was worried, although I don't think she ever knew the full risk."

Nikki squeezed her eyes shut. If Carlton had been involved, Erin was undoubtedly dead. The man had been convicted of three murders but according to news reports, there had been countless more. He must have been furious at her father for his deception. "So Erin might have paid the price," she said slowly.

"Possibly. But you can't put all the blame on your father. He was just doing his best, trying to climb the police ranks."

Robert was too quick to assume she blamed her father. In fact, it helped to understand that there might have been a reason behind Erin's disappearance, that the abduction would have happened regardless of any trail ride. It also confirmed her trust in Justin, no matter that he didn't want to detail every minute of that afternoon. Best of all, she finally had a workable theory, something to pursue.

"I have to see Carlton," she said.

"He'll never agree to that. He was reclusive before. He's probably even more so now. And he's still dangerous."

"I'm going to talk to him. Even if I have to pretend to be someone else."

"That's illegal. You could lose your license. And what's the point? He'll never admit anything. And it's dangerous to go poking at a viper."

Maybe, Nikki thought, but some things were worth the risk. She had to see him, along with Carlton's former wife who might be persuaded to throw a little dirt. Fake credentials might be required but knowing how and when to bluff was an important part of being an investigator. Robert had taught her that.

She jammed the phone between her ear and shoulder, adrenaline pumping, fingers flying over the keyboard as she tapped in Thomas Carlton's name.

"You're not listening to me, are you?" Robert said. "I hear your computer clicking. Ease up. I have a friend who knows the warden. But I'd feel better about calling in favors if you had more than a hunch."

She'd like something more solid too. Admittedly, Carlton might not have had anything to do with Erin's disappearance. After all, her father would have been dead for almost a decade before he sought retribution. Certainly the detectives in charge of Erin's case had never considered her father's job a factor. But short of a crystal ball, there was no real way of knowing.

Her fingers stilled over the keys, her gaze shooting to the door. She didn't have a crystal ball but she did have a loyal friend only thirty feet down the hall. Of course, soliciting psychic help was something she avoided. The last time Sonja had been far from helpful. Her musings about "concrete" and "corner" had been nebulous, and then she had crushed Nikki's hope, suggesting Erin was dead.

This was different though. This wasn't about finding Erin or expecting Sonja to come up with her sister's whereabouts. This was merely checking to see if Carlton had been involved. A simple question really: *Was the man so vindictive he would kill an innocent teen because of her deceased father's undercover job?*

Surely any psychic could handle that.

CHAPTER TWENTY

"FOR AN ACCURATE READING," Sonja said, "I'll need something more than a name. Can I talk to this guy on the phone?"

"Impossible." Nikki settled into one of the wicker chairs and flipped open her laptop. "Carlton is serving consecutive life sentences. Can't you just look at his picture or something? I found a couple on the Internet."

"Some psychics do it that way but it's not my strength."

Nikki leaned forward, still pumped by the idea that Sonja could help, even if she was an unconventional resort. "Can't you pick up on something, some sort of vibe related to Erin? Something, anything, that I can pass on to Robert?"

"If this is to gain Robert's help, whatever I see won't make a bit of difference." Sonja gave a tinkling laugh. "He doesn't believe in psychometry. He's more closed off than you."

"But this *is* for me. So I'll feel better about asking him for another favor. He doesn't have as many contacts now and prison access won't be easy. It's likely Carlton won't admit to anything even if we're able to meet. But I have to try."

"So you believe in my abilities?" Sonja asked. "Or only when I say something you want to hear?"

Nikki gave a rueful nod, acknowledging how she'd stormed out when Sonja stated Erin was no longer alive. For sure, she hadn't wanted to hear that. But Carlton's involvement changed everything...if he actually had been involved.

"You're right," she said, openly grinning now. "But I am trying to be more receptive to what you do. I truly am."

Sonja softened. "Of course I'll help you and Robert. Everything has energy, including photos. But I need a good picture of Carlton, one where he's alone and relaxed."

Nikki was already scrolling over her laptop. She'd bookmarked several images of Carlton: one of him and his wife posing at the races, one outside the court room, and another when he was flanked by his entourage. But it might take awhile to find a candid shot. The man had been reclusive before going to jail and he'd also had plenty of money to pay for protection.

Sonja rose. The scent of freshly brewed coffee filled the room but Nikki stayed focused on finding a useable image. She wasn't sure how long she sat, but her coffee was cold when she finally took a sip.

"I can't find anything," she said, blowing out a sigh. "Carlton didn't even get his picture taken when his horses won."

Which proved he was a stone-cold killer capable of executing an innocent teen. Because who wouldn't get excited about winning? She'd never forget her day at the track when she and Justin had rushed to the winner's circle to greet his victorious horse. She'd been euphoric over the horse's success, totally caught up in the event and for a rare moment, free of guilt about Erin. It had been a liberating afternoon, away from her mother and Robert.

Alone with Justin. Of course, Lara had been with them as well. Obviously she was another of Justin's longtime friends. Maybe even a longtime lover.

Nikki set her mug on the table. Justin and Lara's relationship wasn't her concern. Not today anyway. Right now, all she wanted was a good picture of Thomas Carlton. For a purpose she didn't really believe in.

"I can't believe I'm asking for psychic help," Nikki said, shaking her head and smiling at the same time.

"But this is progress," Sonja said. "It shows you're more accepting of what the universe sends. Now it'll be easier for you to move through the grief stages. And get on with your life."

Nikki rolled her eyes. Just the fact that she was sitting here—asking Sonja to pull energy from a picture—proved she was as open as anyone. It was certainly empowering to finally have a suspect. She'd learned a lot about watching for little tells and she needed to see Carlton's reaction when she asked about Erin. A prison visit would likely be a long time coming. The man was still elusive despite being behind bars. She couldn't even find a suitable photo.

"Here." Sonja pressed a deck of tarot cards in Nikki's hand. "Give them a shuffle. If I can't see Carlton at least I can give you a reading."

"That won't help," Nikki said. But she dutifully shuffled the deck then waited while Sonja dealt three cards face down.

"Does anything in the deck have a prison picture on it?" Nikki joked. "Maybe we could use that."

Sonja turned over the first card and the smile fell from Nikki's face. "The Devil," she breathed, staring at the card. Obviously it represented Carlton. The only thing it didn't have was the man's prison number.

Sonja flipped over more cards. Some of the images were colorful and rather pretty but most were dark. Nikki had no idea what they meant so she focused on watching her friend's reaction. Sonja's mouth had pursed and she kept reaching for the deck, placing more cards below the top three.

"I'm trying to clarify the Three Fates," Sonja said, her voice so low it seemed she was talking more to herself.

"Sounds impressive." Nikki forced a laugh, determined to lighten the mood. But it was hard not to be subdued by the ominous spread of cards. "Do they always look so foreboding?"

Sonja didn't answer. She flipped over another card. This one had a naked man and woman. Despite her skepticism about the reading, Nikki immediately felt better. The man and woman looked young and sexy and definitely happy.

"That's the angel Raphael," Sonja said, turning over another card. The next one wasn't nearly as nice. In fact, it showed a bunch of swords in someone's back.

Sonja abruptly leaned forward and grabbed Nikki's hand. "You have to be careful."

Nikki frowned at the card. She didn't have to be a trained psychic to see that it represented betrayal. Carlton obviously believed he'd been betrayed. But her father had been working on the side of the law and Carlton was a vicious murderer. The man deserved to have ten swords stuck in his back.

"Be careful who you trust," Sonja said, squeezing Nikki's hand with a surprisingly strong grip.

"You always say that."

"Yes, and I'm saying it again." Sonja scooped up the cards, her movements jerky. "Is there a new guy in your life? What about the K-9 man? Do you trust him? What's his name?"

"Tony Lambert. And he's just a work friend."

"No, something's changed. You've been wearing a lovestruck look. And that could make you oblivious to danger. Keep Gunner close when you're around this new guy, even if it ends up in the bedroom."

Nikki shifted, crossing her arms then her legs. It wasn't Tony who she wanted in her bed. It was Justin. And Gunner would be no protection against him. She didn't believe in all this mumbo jumbo stuff but the question came out anyway. "Did you see anything else in the cards? Something that says who I'll be naked with?"

"The cards are open to interpretation," Sonja said. "But it appears you're safe with Tony unless you've met him before. What scares me is that the betrayal was past and future."

"You mean that some guy betrayed me before?"

"Yes," Sonja said.

"How long ago?" Nikki braced her shoulders, dreading the answer.

"Not sure. The betrayal could have been in one of your past lives."

"Past lives? Oh, okay." Nikki refrained from rolling her eyes. She shouldn't have imagined this psychic stuff could help. On the other hand, if it made Sonja happy there was no reason not to indulge her friend and accept the occasional reading. It hadn't been too painful. Although it would be better to do the tarot thing at Vinny's where they could enjoy coffee and biscotti. That would be a better use of their time.

"No matter what you believe or don't believe," Sonja scolded, clearly picking up on Nikki's skepticism, "the betrayal is real. Just remember, you're not alone. You have people who love you and who will always have your back."

She rose and wrapped Nikki in an uncomfortably long hug. When Sonja finally lowered her arms and stepped back, her eyes were twinkling. "I do find it curious that your only question involved your love life."

Sex life, Nikki thought, not love life. And that was because she didn't want to hear Sonja talk about concrete again. Carlton might have attached Erin to a heavy block and dropped her in the water, just as he'd done to one of his competitors. The realization colored a whole new set of images. And the memory of Savannah's dripping blond hair—so similar to Erin's—made her shudder.

"I do believe you'll find her," Sonja said, turning serious. "And that you'll finally be able to give her a proper burial."

Always before Nikki had rejected the suggestion that Erin was dead but now she only nodded. "That's what I'm hoping for," she said.

CHAPTER TWENTY-ONE

NIKKI SPEED-DIALED Justin's phone then lost her nerve and jabbed the red button. She hadn't talked to him in days, not since their visit to the K-9 center. But it was obvious he wasn't going to call her. It would have been easier to apologize for doubting him if they hadn't shared that kiss. Now the lines were uncomfortably blurred.

She leaned over her office chair and stroked Gunner's head, always her go-to response when battling indecision. Calling Justin and telling him about Carlton's link to Erin would certainly be normal. Her sister's disappearance had always been the tie that bound them. But she wanted Justin to know he was more than that. Contacting him now, only to reveal she needed help with a new suspect, would only cheapen her apology.

Gunner tilted his head so she could reach behind his ear, and she gave him another preoccupied scratch. Dogs were much easier to understand than men. Give Gunner a bone, a little attention and everything was forgiven, no matter her offense.

Of course, men appreciated food too.

Brightening, she picked up her phone and called Vinny. It was early evening and the restaurant would be busy, but she had no doubt he'd be happy to pack something to go.

Thirty minutes later, she was weaving through traffic with the mouth-watering smell of Italian food filling her car. She glanced at the thermal bag on her front seat and then in the rearview mirror at Gunner. He was drooling, his eyes locked on the bag. She had no idea what Vinny had packed but clearly it had her dog's approval. With his keen sense of smell, he probably knew every type of cheese and seasonings.

"We may not get any of this food," she warned. Justin might not be home or he could have already eaten. Or he might have company. But it didn't matter if Lara or some other woman was there. Nikki wanted to apologize.

She'd hurt him with her questions and her belief in his innocence had little to do with the emergence of Carlton as a likely suspect. Justin helped people; he didn't hurt them. Certainly his focus was on punishing wrongdoers but that punishment stayed within legal boundaries. He'd always had a deep respect for life, from safety at the barn to the health of people and horses to worrying about all the unwanted animals dumped at the end of the driveway.

She turned onto a residential street, peering through the dusk at the stately homes. Street lights illuminated the sidewalk but they weren't much help revealing house numbers. Justin had moved from his city condo several years ago. She'd been to his home on a few occasions. He'd always been driving though and she hadn't paid much attention. In fact, she'd barely made it past the front door. There had been the time when he'd made her coffee and she had used a downstairs bathroom, but she couldn't remember many details, just an overall impression of masculine luxury.

She'd assumed he didn't want dog hair all over his house but that didn't make sense considering he'd kept Gunner here for six months. And he didn't brush at his pants like some people did, as if dog hairs were a form of kryptonite. He certainly hadn't minded Gunner in his car. Then again, Justin was a difficult man to understand.

Gunner whined and she checked the rearview mirror. He was standing now, no longer eyeing the food. His nose was pressed against the side window as he stared at a large house set back from the street. It looked somewhat familiar. She definitely remembered the wooden fence extending from the side. She didn't covet many things but a big fenced yard was on that list.

She eased to a stop alongside the curb. A scattering of vehicles dotted the street. None of them were Justin's but that didn't mean he wasn't home. His house had a triple garage. And even though she'd told herself she didn't care if Lara was visiting, it was a relief to see there wasn't a horse trailer parked in his drive.

She scooped up the food and swung open her door.

"Stay," she said, leaving the car and air conditioner running. It would be presumptuous to knock on the door with Gunner at her side, considering she wasn't at all sure of her welcome. Likely this would be an Uber-style delivery. And if Justin wasn't there, she and Gunner would simply drive home and enjoy a lavish Italian meal. Not such a bad outcome except then she'd have to figure out another way to apologize.

She took a moment to lower the side window, an ingrained safety habit. This didn't seem a neighborhood of muggers but she hadn't forgotten Sonja's warning to keep him close. If Gunner needed to come to her rescue he'd be able to leap from the car and be at her side in seconds.

"Stay," she repeated, then turned and strode up the flagstone walkway, too preoccupied to enjoy the beautiful orange trees and the scent of night-blooming jasmine.

She pressed the doorbell, holding Vinny's thermal bag in front of her like a shield. Her nervousness was surprising. She wasn't a people pleaser, and she and Justin often disagreed. But this was different. She'd hurt him and the knowledge weighed heavy.

She automatically assessed his security: steel door, sensor lights and at least one visible camera. Quite a fortress. She pressed the doorbell again but the time dragged, long enough for her to locate two more subtle cameras. Obviously he could see who was at the front door so he must not be home. Or he didn't want to answer.

Her shoulders sagged the same time as the heavy door swung open. The first thing she noticed was Justin's rumpled hair, his bare feet, his scowl. Oh, hell, he must have a female guest. Even grumpy, he looked totally hot.

"What's wrong?" he asked.

"Nothing," she said, trying not to gape at the ripples beneath his tight shirt. He must have intensified his workouts since she'd last seen him at the gym. She didn't remember him being so bulked up, or maybe she was just hyper conscious now. She pulled her gaze upward and shoved the bag out so forcefully it hit his flat stomach.

"Is this some sort of clue?" he asked, still frowning.

"No, it's food," she said. "Part of my apology. I'm sorry for thinking so crazy, you know, about Erin. It's always been easier to blame you than m-me." She paused, surprised at the lump in her throat and how it was making her voice crack. She studied his face, searching for any hint of softening. His mouth was still flat but at least he hadn't slammed the door in her face.

Swallowing, she forged on. "You're right about old baggage. Erin's probably always going to be my hot spot. But I need to stop jumping to conclusions, letting it drive my life, and interfering with, you know, important relationships."

"It's okay, Nikki." His voice sounded too resigned to make her feel much better. However he did reach out a chiseled arm and take the food, and she caught the flare of his nostrils. "Smells good," he said. "Is it from Vinny's?"

"Yes, and there's lots. Enough for a family of four. He's always giving extra." She pressed her mouth shut, didn't want to sound like she was trying to extract an invitation. Worse, she was babbling, something she never did.

"Why don't you take some home," he said, peering into the bag. "You're probably hungry too. I don't need all this."

So he was alone. But he didn't want to invite her in.

Not surprising. His home was his refuge—the place to escape the demands of his job—and her conversation always circled back to police topics. She used him as a sounding board for Erin and it was time to ease up. She pulled in a breath, steeling herself for rejection.

"Or we could eat it together," she said. "And I promise not to talk about law enforcement, fighting techniques or my sister."

"Think you can do that?" His skeptical expression made her think a long moment before answering.

"I don't know," she said. "But I'd like to try."

CHAPTER TWENTY-TWO

"TRY SOME MORE CANNELLONI," Nikki said, sliding the cardboard container closer to Justin's plate. "It's Vinny's signature dish."

Gunner glanced up from his spot on the floor, his eyes hopeful. Justin hadn't hesitated about inviting her dog in. As soon as he'd spotted Gunner, he'd strode over and opened the car door.

"No, thanks," Justin said, tapping his stomach. "I'm full. It's a good thing Gunner is around to take care of leftovers."

"I thought you might not want him inside," she said. It was understandable Justin didn't want hair everywhere. His sleek kitchen dissolved into a luxurious den with a Persian rug, copper light fixtures and watercolors displayed over a circular stone fireplace. She was no connoisseur but even the art looked expensive.

"Gunner lived here for a while," Justin said. "He knows the rules."

"Which are?"

"Dogs stay downstairs. No climbing on furniture or unnecessary barking."

Easy enough. Gunner certainly didn't look inclined to break them, not like at Robert's where he kept sneaking into the pool area. Although if dogs were so graciously accepted, it meant *she* was the one who had never ranked an invite.

"I remember your last place," she said, working hard to keep the wistfulness from her voice. "We always used to barbecue after our workouts."

"Yes."

"It was fun."

He nodded.

"And you had that detector to check beneath cars," she said.

"Yes."

She cradled her wine glass, trying to think of a way to draw him out—a way that didn't veer into police talk. There was definitely a wall between them, and it was even more apparent now that they'd finished eating. He was doling out words like they were blocks of gold and she longed for their old camaraderie. "You've been here for what...two years?" she asked.

"Five."

"Oh, I didn't realize it was that long."

"You've been focused."

She shot him a wary look. Was that a polite way of saying she'd been obsessed with finding Erin? But she wasn't going to apologize. At one time, he'd been similarly obsessed. They'd certainly never struggled for conversation before. Of course, always before they had Erin to talk about. And when Nikki had been a kid at the barn, they'd been busy discussing horses.

She'd promised not to talk about police work but horses seemed a safe subject, so long as it didn't lead back to the stable. Questions still nagged at her about that day, like if Pancho had been cut by spurs. But she pressed her lips together, realizing that staying on safe topics was rather difficult. And it was quite a revelation that she couldn't go thirty minutes without talking about her sister.

A smile played over Justin's mouth. Clearly he'd picked up on her frustration. But that was okay because his amusement was far better than disinterested one-word replies.

"I've been a pain, haven't I?" She reached over and squeezed his hand. "I understand that no one wants to talk about old cases. The other detectives stopped returning my calls ages ago."

He moved his hand out from beneath hers and reached for the wine bottle. "That's because you remind us of our failures. And even cops need to escape those for a while."

She gave a silent wince. Despite her best intentions, she'd pushed the conversation back into work. Worse, she'd done it inside his home, his sanctuary from the horrors of his job.

"I'll always return your calls," he went on. "Your loyalty and fire is admirable. Don't ever lose that. I just wish you'd ease up on the witch hunts. I never know what direction you're running."

His words were level but there was an edge to his voice. He'd never asked her to ease up. In fact, countless times he'd helped her and Robert check out fringe suspects: the hiker who happened to have a criminal record, the vet student who had visited the barn, and the male librarian who'd found Erin a history book and given her his private number.

"You never called them witch hunts before," Nikki said. "Only after I asked where you were at four o'clock that day. If our positions were reversed, I'd certainly expect questions. And answers. I am an investigator after all, something you encouraged me to become." Sighing, she set down her glass. "But I'm talking about Erin again. Seems I can't stop. So I'll go now."

"I was moving shavings from the pit to the shed that day," Justin said tonelessly. "That's where I was between four and four-thirty."

Shock froze her. That was a lie, and not a very good one. Justin had never wasted time with bedding. That was the handyman's job; shavings were trucked in every Saturday morning when stable workers—kids like her and Erin—were around to shovel. Then through the week they moved the shavings to the back of the barn as required for the stalls.

But there had been shavings stockpiled at the end of the barn. She remembered her relief when she saw she didn't have to push a wheelbarrow back and forth to the outside pit. It had sped up her job, leaving her time to practice braiding. *Had Justin done that?* She shook her head in confusion. "Why?"

"You were a spunky little kid," he said. "But cleaning all those stalls for your sister was wearing you down. I thought you needed help."

That made sense. He'd always helped anyone who was struggling. But she hadn't been asking why he'd done it, but why hadn't he told her in the car when she had asked. It was almost as if he was embarrassed. The truth would have cleared everything up though, and the trip to the K-9 facility might have ended differently. And much more pleasurably.

She tilted her head, her eyes narrowing.

"I gave a complete accounting of my time to the police," Justin added dryly. "And there were other people that confirmed my whereabouts. So you can stop looking at me like I'm a suspect."

The fact that other people had confirmed his whereabouts didn't jive with the information in her office file, but re-stocking the shavings explained a lot. And the relief that warmed her chest was more than welcome. "You never really were a suspect," she said. "Besides, I have a new name. I'll tell you about him another day."

This time it was Justin who grabbed her hand. "Tell me now. It's dangerous for you to be chasing these leads alone."

"Okay," she said happily. She always liked to talk about this stuff with Justin and the fact that he was holding her hand made it even better. "His name is Thomas Carlton. He's doing life for drug running, money laundering and murder. Turns out my father was one of the cops who played a part in his conviction. And Carlton had a habit of making people disappear. Of getting even."

"Carlton was big money at the track," Justin said slowly. "But that was a long time ago and he's been locked up for years. Long before Erin disappeared."

"Yes, but what if he was biding his time? Waiting to take his revenge?"

"Doesn't feel right. And previous investigators never believed there was a link. But it's true your father was the keystone of that case. His evidence was invaluable."

There it was again. Someone praising her father. And though Justin didn't realize it, his hand was still wrapped around hers, his touch both exciting and soothing. His scowl wasn't soothing though. And it seemed to deepen the more he thought about Carlton.

"I better check." He scrubbed a hand over his jaw. "See if Carlton has any power. Find out if he had a vendetta for your family."

"But there's no one left in my family. Only me."

"Exactly," Justin said.

CHAPTER TWENTY-THREE

NIKKI STRETCHED BACK against the sofa, her left hand trailing over Gunner's head, the other cupping the glass of wine Justin kept filled. It had been a long time since she'd felt so relaxed. Not talking about Erin wasn't so difficult. In fact, she hadn't mentioned the case in almost an hour, not since Justin promised to check up on Carlton. Knowing he was following up was a big relief. She'd already made an appointment to visit Carlton's ex-wife so between the two of them they had things under control.

Admittedly, the dinner and wine contributed to her sense of well-being but it wasn't only that. Justin was back to his old self, and they talked about everything from politics and sports to the best vacation hiking trails. He'd traveled much more than her; his art pieces had been picked up in various countries. He was also still a passionate horse lover. One of his walls was entirely devoted to race pictures.

"I like the picture of the two horses in the stretch," she said. "Where one wants to win so much, he's reaching over to bite."

"That's Great Prospector, doing anything he can to cross the wire first." The approval in Justin's voice showed he empathized with the horse trying to intimidate his rival.

"The horses are certainly competitive," she said. "It was obvious that time you took me to the races. That day was so much fun."

"Then why did you refuse to come with me again?"

She was about to shrug it off but his eyes were intent, as if her answer was important. "I felt guilty," she said. "Having fun, laughing, forgetting. Mom wasn't pleased when I came home..." She let her voice trail off, determined not to mention Erin's name and wreck the evening.

"Your mom was probably sensitive about the track," Justin said. "Your father spent a lot of time there."

"You mean when he was working the Carlton case?"

"No, he was always a big race fan. He even founded a Thoroughbred ownership group. It's been over twenty years and officers are still having fun with it."

"But we didn't have money like that." She tilted her head in confusion. "Certainly not enough to own a racehorse."

"Ownership consortiums don't cost much. Anyone can buy in with a modest investment. That's how I got started. Five hundred bucks and I was the proud owner of a chestnut mare called Beginner's Luck." His laugh was rich and deep, as if the memory still brought pleasure. "Me and twenty-nine other cops."

"But there was never any horse talk at our house. Mom didn't like horses. She was so upset when I went to the track with you that day. It was easier to just avoid horses considering the way she yelled. And all the other stuff she dredged up."

Nikki felt disrespectful, speaking about her mother, remembering her tirades. But Justin simply wrapped an arm around her shoulder. His touch was reassuring, as was his silence. He never asked questions about her relationship with her mom; he already knew.

"I have a picture of your dad at the track," he said after a moment. "I bought a yearling by one of Carlton's stallions and the manager sent me some photos from the stud's stakes wins. It must have been taken when your dad was posing as a groom. Want me to pull it out?"

A week ago she would have spurned the offer but now she hesitated. Part of her reluctance came from their position on the sofa. Justin had shifted so that his arm draped over the back of the couch but his hand still rested on her shoulder. And she wasn't in a hurry for him to move.

"That picture must have been early in the investigation," she said. "Because I already learned that Dad was a driver for Carlton. That's how he was able to tape all the incriminating conversations. I'm meeting with Carlton's ex-wife tomorrow, see what she remembers. Based on our phone call, it sounds as if she doesn't like him much."

Justin's hand tightened over her shoulder, his grip a warning. "Be careful poking around. Carlton might be protective. I know his brother is still active. Their organization isn't the powerhouse it once was, but it still has bite. When I talk to the warden, I'll find out who's on Carlton's visitor list. See if his ex stays in touch. She may not be entirely truthful."

"When will you talk to the warden?"

"Tomorrow," Justin said.

She twisted in surprise. Robert thought any warden talks would take weeks, if not months. Clearly Justin had more clout. He'd always been a staunch friend, never worrying about calling in favors on her behalf and always interested in her life. Yet he had interests like horse racing she hadn't even known about.

It was as if she'd been wearing blinkers all these years. Certainly she'd participated in many activities with him—martial arts, conditioning and visiting the shooting range—but those had been driven by her goal to find Erin. She'd also refused to talk about her father and that close-mindedness in someone else would have left her frustrated. But that was going to change.

"Yes." She gave a smiling nod. "I'd love to see that picture of Dad."

Justin squeezed her shoulder, rose and disappeared into what looked like an office, judging by the partially visible bookcase.

He returned with a thick binder. "There might be pictures from the riding stable mixed in," he warned.

She nodded. It had been her mother, not her, who had cleansed their home of every photo containing a horse, or a picture of her father. Her mom had been forever thrusting albums at Robert, pleading for him to get rid of them. Justin had been privy to some of her mother's rants and even one pointed reference that Erin's abductor must have worked at the stable. Nikki had been horrified and embarrassed, and clearly Justin remembered.

"It'll be good to see *all* the pictures," she said with a smile.

And it was. In fact, it was rather cathartic flipping through the pages, listening to Justin's deep voice introducing her to the various horses he'd known. His family had owned horses since he was a kid, but he hadn't been drawn into racing until his first year as a rookie cop.

Halfway through the album, he stopped, pointing out Carlton's horse. She barely twitched when he tapped the decades-old picture of her father grinning from the winner's circle, looking impossibly young and full of vitality.

"Hard to believe he was working undercover," she said, studying her father's cocky grin. It wasn't just the coloring she'd inherited from him, but also his eyes and mouth.

"Apparently he was good at his job," Justin said. "The first from his class to make it into undercover."

"Sometimes I wish he hadn't," she said, surprised by the empathy she felt for her father. She hadn't had much sympathy before, deciding he'd been a coward for giving up on life. "Maybe if he hadn't been exposed to all that darkness, he'd still be alive."

"It's a tough job," Justin said. "I'm sure your mother wasn't comfortable with him disappearing for weeks at a time. The best can burn out, no matter how much support they receive at home."

Or how little. Nikki doubted her mother had been super supportive. Although she remembered the laughter when her parents were together; they'd seemed happy. Her mother had been so quiet after he died. The sniping and blame pointing hadn't started until after Erin disappeared. Looking at her father's confident face, remembering his infectious laugh, made it hard to believe that short months later he would take his own life.

She traced her finger over the picture. He looked carefree, a victorious groom standing in the winner's circle beside Carlton's horse. But he must have been terrified that his identity would be exposed. Maybe it had. Perhaps he hadn't chosen to leave his life, his family...her.

"Is there any possibility Carlton got to him?" She kept her voice light, knowing she was grasping. The coroner had ruled it a suicide; her father had been found slumped over a park bench with his gun in his hand. He'd been thoughtful though, making sure there was no mess in their home. And that his body would be quickly discovered by a beat cop.

She felt Justin's narrowed gaze. "There was never a note," she added.

"I never realized you had doubts." His arm tightened, pulling her closer. "You never said anything before."

"I never spoke about him before. And I didn't know about the Carlton case. Not until Tony mentioned it."

"Fair enough," Justin said. "Want me to take a look?"

"You always do so much. I didn't come here for that."

He tilted her face, his eyes boring into hers. "Then why did you come?"

Her pulse was racing so fast he probably felt it pounding beneath his thumb. But she'd never been one for games and besides, Justin always knew when she was avoiding the truth.

"I wanted to see you," she said simply. And so that there was no doubt, she added, "To be with you."

His eyes remained locked on hers even as he pried the wine glass from her fingers. His other hand still cupped her face, his gaze so intent she shivered with anticipation. He must have felt her reaction because his eyes darkened. When he spoke, his voice was thick. "Go to the kitchen, Gunner," he said.

Gunner rose, his nails clicking over the hardwood floor. He thumped down in the kitchen, his sigh loud and resigned, as if he understood what was about to transpire on the sofa. And that he wasn't totally enthused. Clearly he'd been banished before.

"He knows the drill," she said. But she didn't want to think about Justin's other women. Not now. Because his mouth had lowered over hers, his kiss even hungrier than it had been last week. But this time his hand slipped beneath her shirt, and the way he handled her breasts left her melting.

Or maybe it was his other hand, the one that was stroking the inside of her thighs that was turning her buttery soft with want. Her skyrocketing desire surprised her and she fumbled at his belt. And then he was helping her, sliding off both their pants and tossing them aside.

Moments later she was naked on the couch, his big body posed over her. She had the fleeting thought that he'd mastered both speed and efficiency, no doubt because he never knew when he'd be called in. Obviously he'd trained Gunner to vacate the room. But that was okay. It meant he knew his way around a woman's body and tonight she'd be the beneficiary of all that experience.

She closed her eyes, pushing away thoughts of anyone but Justin. Condom foil crinkled but not much else was happening. She gave an impatient wiggle and opened her eyes.

He was staring at her face, unmoving. "You're wrong," he whispered.

"Wrong about what?" She wrapped her arms around his neck, tugging him closer, trying to hurry him up. She could feel his hardness, could tell his urgency matched hers. But he remained still, his mouth frustratingly far away.

"I know what you think Gunner is telling you," he said. "But this isn't my usual drill. You need to know that."

"Let's talk about your drill afterwards," she said.

Smiling, he let her pull him to her. But she heard his words even as he filled her with that first hard thrust.

"I always make it to the bedroom," he said, his mouth against her neck. "Just not with you, Nik. Only you."

CHAPTER TWENTY-FOUR

NIKKI WOKE TO THE SOUND of running water. She reached across the bed, drowsily searching for Justin, even though it had to be him in the shower. She hadn't heard him get up, rather remarkable since she couldn't remember a moment throughout the night when they hadn't been entwined.

Even more surprising was that she'd slept so deeply. Even with her longest-ever boyfriend—all of five months—she'd never been able to fall asleep beside him, often moving to the couch so she could catch some sleep. He'd complained she had trust issues.

Clearly that hadn't been a problem last night. Maybe it had been the intense physical activity that had let her sleep so well. Or maybe it was because of Justin's huge bed with the luxurious satin sheets. More likely it was how he'd touched every inch of her body, finding erogenous zones in the most interesting places. No getting around it, he was a virtual sex god. And last night, he'd made her feel like a goddess.

The first time the sex had been hot and explosive, almost primal in their urgency. She'd thought they were both satisfied. Then he'd scooped her up from the sofa, carried her upstairs and demonstrated the full range of his talents. And she'd responded with moves she didn't know she possessed.

She stretched, her mouth curving in a dreamy smile. The smell of sandalwood soap drifted through the room. She opened her eyes.

Justin stood beside her. Water sparkled over his ripped chest and a white towel was wrapped around his hips. She reached for him, inhaling his masculine scent, but he remained several feet away. He didn't speak, just stared with an odd expression. Was he regretting their night?

"Good morning," she said, the words almost a question.

"It's a fucking fantastic morning." He spoke with such fervor it was clear she'd misjudged his silence.

She grinned up at him, her gaze lowering to the growing bulge beneath his towel. "Glad you feel that way," she said, reaching for him. "Best of all, it looks like you're not finished yet. Surprising really, considering..."

"I'll never be finished with you." He captured her hand before she could tug off the towel, then stooped, covering her mouth with a hard kiss. "But dammit, I have to go."

"Surely you can stay a few more minutes," she murmured. Already her nipples were tightening, her body reacting to his touch. Clearly it wasn't just her mind that remembered. And all he was doing was holding her hand.

"Had a call," he said. "But how about dinner tonight? I can make a reservation somewhere."

"Or we could just eat here."

He skimmed his mouth over the back of her wrist. "Good. That will give us more time."

The way he growled the word "time" made her clench with anticipation. She didn't really want to wait though and it might be possible to tug off his towel. Lingering in bed would be far more fun than getting up this early. Obviously though, a phone call meant he was needed and justice was more important than satisfying their leftover lust.

She shoved away the sheet and swung her legs over the bed. "I'll be quick. I just need a second to get dressed."

"No need to get up. I'll put Gunner in the backyard so you can sleep. I wrote down the door codes so you won't get locked out." His gaze swept over her breasts and then back to her face. "I'll call you later. And next time park in the garage where your car is safer."

He strode into his dressing room, leaving her stunned and still gripping the sheet. She must have misunderstood. His home was his private domain. More than one of his girlfriends had complained that he never let them stay, booting them out of his bed and house whenever he received a work call. She'd thought that was very reasonable. Like her, Justin probably brought home confidential files and she didn't want sleepover company wandering around, poking their noses in places they shouldn't.

But he hadn't only invited her to stay; he was leaving her his security codes. To the front. To the back. To his garage.

She let her head sink back on the pillow, absorbing the luxury of sleeping late. She couldn't remember the last time she'd done that. Definitely before she had Gunner who was always quite insistent that he be taken outside at the crack of dawn.

Justin's steps sounded as he descended the stairs, then she heard his voice as he greeted Gunner. There was no sound of a back door opening but the kitchen was on the opposite side of the house. She couldn't make out his words either, just a low rumble, but the fact that he was still talking to Gunner left her feeling all warm inside.

She rolled onto her side and flipped the pillow over her head, determined to grab this rare opportunity when she didn't have to tend to her dog. But she was wide awake now, too focused on the sounds in the house. Maybe it was best to get up too. She still had to prepare questions for her interview with Carlton's ex. She'd wait for Justin to drive off and then retrieve her clothes.

She propped up against the headboard, listening for more sounds. But the house was silent. Maybe he'd already put Gunner in the backyard and driven away. Surely she'd have heard something though, even if it was just the vibrating garage door.

She slipped out from beneath the sheets, walked to the window and pushed back the curtain. A reddish sun peeked over the horizon but the residential street was still dark and empty. Movement flashed and she spotted her dog.

Gunner wasn't in the back yard but loose on Justin's front lawn. He sniffed then raised his leg and peed on some decorative shrubs. She pressed closer to the glass, peering in dismay. Did he jump the fence? Then she realized he wasn't alone. Justin was kneeling behind her back bumper, feeling beneath her car.

He searched the undercarriage for another moment then rose, brushed off his pants and strode around the side of the house. Gunner bounded after him and they disappeared from sight. Moments later, a garage door whirred and Justin's black SUV rolled down the driveway.

Shaking her head, she let the curtain fall into place. Detectives were a suspicious bunch and Justin's paranoia about her car emphasized the nature of his job. Robert and Justin had wanted her to rent a house with a garage, citing security reasons. However, she didn't have to worry about sabotage. Unlike Justin, she hadn't put anyone behind bars. Her most significant contribution had been Savannah's case. And Matthew Friedel wasn't the sort to plant tracking devices or bombs beneath cars.

Thomas Carlton was though.

She shook away that thought almost as soon as it popped in her head. She hadn't roused Carlton's antipathy yet, other than to call his ex-wife and arrange a visit. Besides, if someone tampered with her car it would mean she was moving closer to finding Erin's abductor. That would be a welcome development. Because when killers were threatened, they took action. And action often led to answers.

She hurried into the bathroom and enjoyed a quick shower, relieved to see only masculine shampoo on Justin's shelves. He may entertain other women but he didn't encourage them to leave feminine products on display. She used the new toothbrush he'd left by the sink, resisting the temptation to peek into his cupboards. He'd removed any visible signs of other ladies and that thoughtful gesture was enough.

She wrapped herself in an oversized towel and headed downstairs, eager to see Gunner. Her clothes has been gathered and left on the sofa, and she dressed quickly. A sheet of paper listing the codes lay on the counter and she scooped it up before stepping out the back door.

Gunner was posed by the fence, staring up at a scolding gray squirrel. At the click of the door, he wheeled and trotted onto the deck, happy to see her but not as exuberant as she'd expected. He gave her hand a hasty lick, then wheeled and raced back to the fence, hopeful the squirrel would eventually come to ground.

He was in for a long wait, but the squirrel was excellent entertainment. Gunner was trained not to bark gratuitously so there was no reason not to enjoy a cup of Justin's coffee before she left.

She entered the security code on the keypad and stepped back into the house.

The sleek coffee maker was more complicated than the ones she was used to, but the brew it produced was dark and strong. Too strong. Sputtering, she opened his fridge and added a splash of milk. Justin must have a cast-iron stomach. Like his body.

She allowed herself a shiver of pleasure before straightening her thoughts. There was much to do. If Justin used his pull with the warden, it was possible she'd see Carlton very soon. Even reclusive prisoners tended to meet with visitors, if only to break the mindless monotony. She needed to think about her questions as well as the best way to conceal her identity. She didn't expect much cooperation; even Sonja's tarot cards confirmed Carlton was the devil.

Maybe she could pretend to be researching one of Carlton's Thoroughbreds; Justin had said one of his stallions had been a top ten sire. But Carlton might blame horses for his conviction. After all, it had been his passion for racing that had let the undercover cops—primarily her father—gain his confidence. Maybe it would be better to say she was working on a book about wrongful imprisonment and how families coped with the fallout. She'd have a better idea of the best angle after meeting with Carlton's ex today.

She scanned the kitchen for a pen, keen to jot down her ideas. However the counters were clear of everything except the spoon she'd used to stir her coffee. Justin was definitely much tidier than she was.

She checked the den but his neatness was evident there as well. Their wine glasses from last night had disappeared, along with the photo album. She didn't know when he'd had a chance to tidy up. Certainly he hadn't done it last night and there would have been little time this morning. Maybe he'd returned downstairs while she was sleeping. She knew he moved like a ninja but the idea that he'd been awake while she'd been oblivious left her feeling unsettled.

She glanced through the doorway of his office but there weren't any pens on the desk. In fact, everything appeared to be locked away. A steel gun safe stood in the far corner and a long table was lined with file boxes. She'd expected to see crime photos pinned up, but the wallboards were blank. The pictures hanging on the left were related to horse racing, not law enforcement. That must be his escape wall, something good to see after staring too long at grisly photos.

She inched into the office, drawn by the pictures and the chance to gain more insight into Justin outside of his work persona.

He'd definitely downplayed his success at the track. His horses had run in very prestigious races, judging by the big smiles and even bigger purses. One photo showed more than thirty people beaming from the winner's circle, probably one of the ownership groups he'd mentioned. He certainly had a wide variety of friends. Some had an unmistakable cop look; others appeared as if they'd just stepped off a wanted poster.

She was about to back away when a familiar face caught her attention, a face she saw every day in the mirror. There were only four other people standing beside her: Justin, Lara, the trainer and the groom. Everyone looked genuinely happy, except maybe Lara who was smiling like a bridesmaid at a wedding. Unlike the other pictures, this race had been a minor one with a very modest purse. But she'd certainly treasured that day. Clearly so had Justin.

She leaned forward, drawn by the striking lines of his face. He was so handsome, looking far more approachable when he was smiling. Actually on closer inspection, his mouth was tilted. Not like Lara's but almost like a snarl concealed behind a smile. He was staring to the left of the photographer, his hand on Nikki's shoulder. Her first thought was that he looked ready to pull her away if the horse jumped. But his eyes were locked on someone beyond the winner's circle.

Who else had been at the races that day? She could only remember Justin picking her up. She'd been disappointed to see Lara lodged in the front seat but also relieved, knowing her mom wouldn't worry so much if there was another woman present. Of course, that hadn't stopped her from launching into another horse tirade as soon as Nikki returned, and that reaction had been the reason she hadn't accepted any more of Justin's invitations.

She stared thoughtfully at the framed photo. Her mom had been suspicious of everyone. Justin had given Nikki a copy of the win picture and—like him—she'd proudly hung it on her wall. But her mother had removed it the very next day, claiming she couldn't bear to look at another horse.

"You can't blame horses for what happened to Dad and Erin," Nikki had said.

"No," her mother snapped. "But I can blame the people around the horses."

Nikki had never seen the picture again.

Sighing, she turned and trudged from the office. Ironically her mother may have been right. Because Thomas Carlton and his horses could be tied to this. And though her mother wasn't alive to see it, it seemed the mystery surrounding Erin's disappearance might finally be solved. And maybe along the way Nikki would learn more about her father.

CHAPTER TWENTY-FIVE

JUSTIN'S NEIGHBORHOOD had sprouted to life, and now Audis and BMWs spilled from the streets, joining the congested arteries that led to the city center. Nikki was filled with too much shimmering energy to mind the traffic. She would have avoided the gridlock if she hadn't lingered so long over coffee, but it had been fun watching Gunner and the squirrel. It had also given her time to formulate the questions she wanted to ask Mrs. Carlton.

Heavy traffic meant it would be quicker to drive directly to her office rather than return home, but that wasn't an issue. She kept dog food and a change of clothes stashed at work in case of long jobs...or memorable evenings like last night.

She smiled in the rearview mirror at Gunner. "Justin's pretty wonderful, isn't he?"

Gunner thumped his tail, either in agreement or simply because of her happy voice. Probably a bit of both.

Her phone chirped. The display showed Robert's cell number and she pressed the green button, tamping down her disappointment that it wasn't Justin.

"Are you on a surveillance job?" Robert asked. "I'm at your office but see your car isn't here. I can't wait any longer. Have to make a nine o'clock tee time."

"I'm driving to the office now." She refrained from saying anything more. Robert had been influenced by her mother, and though he and Justin no longer had much interaction, she sensed his disapproval whenever she mentioned Justin's name.

"I just wanted to update you." Satisfaction deepened Robert's voice. "I spoke to my contact who has a friend with the warden. He's going to help us figure out the best way to get to Carlton. Next month there's a fundraiser that the warden always attends. He'll approach him then."

Nikki winced. She should have texted Robert before he went to all this trouble. But now that Justin was handling it, she no longer had to rely on Robert's convoluted chain of contacts. "I'm so appreciative," she said. "But you don't have to do anything more. Justin is going to arrange a visit. He's going to talk to the warden today."

"Well, that's helpful." Robert gave a rueful chuckle. "Wardens tend to bend over backwards for homicide detectives. But I'm surprised Justin has the time to be bothered with this. And everything has a price. I hope you didn't have to give him too much?"

"Not at all." Her words came out breathy. Only the best night of sex she'd ever had. It was a good thing Robert couldn't see her dopey smile. She cleared her throat. "Justin hasn't forgotten Erin," she said. "Like us, he's never going to quit. He's the one who signed out her police file. It seems Savannah's murder has sparked a renewed interest in all of us."

"That's good," Robert said. "With everyone pushing, something is bound to break."

Her thoughts exactly, and Nikki gave an enthusiastic nod despite knowing Robert couldn't see her. "I'm going to talk to Carlton's ex-wife. See how much she knew about his business. I realize it's a long shot but maybe he had something to do with Dad's death too. Justin is going to take a look at that old file as well."

"It's a possibility," Robert said thoughtfully. "Your father died almost a year after he gave evidence so investigators didn't believe it was related. But at the time no one knew Carlton's brother had taken over." His voice changed, laced with concern. "But it's safer for you to stay away from Carlton's wife until Justin or I can go with you. They may be divorced but you can bet he doesn't want her talking. And he still has access to some very ruthless people."

"Justin gave the same warning." Nikki gunned her car into the left lane, closely following a Volvo wagon. Conversely, Justin respected that she was an investigator. He'd only cautioned her to be careful while Robert tried to shield her. And Robert's way was always too plodding.

"Good," Robert said. "So you'll listen to us. And stay safe." He sounded distracted and she could hear a horn honking in the background.

"Actually I have an interview with Mrs. Carlton this afternoon." Nikki spoke firmly, letting him know she didn't intend to cancel.

"Okay, but take Gunner. And be careful. At least we all know where you are." His voice brightened. "By the way, I came by your office because I found a report containing details about Erin's horse. It was mixed with some of my old files in the attic."

"That's great." But Nikki stared at the car in front of her, fighting off her foreboding. "What did it say?"

"I only scanned it quickly but the horse's registered name was Pancho's Pride. He was sixteen years old and there was something about his size. Something in hands, I think. Does that make sense?"

"Yes, but his height isn't important. What about his condition?" Her voice was sharper than she intended, totally unfair since Robert didn't know much about horses. He'd shared her mother's distaste of everything equine. "Did it mention anything about Pancho's skin? Or hair?"

"Hair? I think the report said he was brown. I just grabbed the one-page summary, not the full report."

"So there was nothing out of the ordinary?" She blew out a sigh of relief.

"That's correct," Robert said. "Just a spot where he'd rubbed his mane along with a couple abrasions."

"Abrasions?" Her foot jerked so abruptly she almost bumped the Volvo ahead of her. "Where were the cuts? On his legs? From the branches maybe?"

"Maybe. But the cuts were on his ribs, not his legs. The report said they were superficial. Certainly not enough to make Erin dismount. Just a little bloody."

Bloody. They had to have been caused by spurs. A buzzing filled her ears and she could barely hear Robert inviting her to drop by tonight and pick up the report. He said something about barbecue but her mind felt molasses slow. She didn't even remember saying goodbye, only knew she was alone in the car with nothing but a silent phone and Gunner whining in her ear.

"Lie down, Gunner. That report doesn't mean a thing." She pushed his head away then instantly felt contrite. He was only trying to help, always quick to pick up on her emotions.

"No need to worry," she added with forced cheerfulness. But that was a bald-faced lie. Because nothing had bothered Justin more than seeing a rider jabbing ineffectually with their spurs. Erin had probably lost her temper when Pancho couldn't keep up to the other riders. She would have been upset, ramming and kicking at her horse's sides, trying to force him across the brook.

Had Justin ridden to the clearing and noticed the blood? Maybe he'd fired her on the spot. If Erin was in one of her moods, she might have mouthed off at him.

That wouldn't have gone over well.

Nikki's hands tightened around the wheel. Of course, Justin wouldn't have intended to hurt anyone. Maybe he'd pulled Erin from the saddle and she'd hit her head. So he'd tried to cover it up. The girth had been loosened and Pancho safely tied. Police concluded it had been Erin who had looked after her horse, running up the stirrups so they wouldn't bump his sides.

But it could have been someone else—a man who cared passionately about animals.

A choke tangled in her throat. Justin had asked her to trust him. And she had, accepting his story that he'd been filling the shavings pile, liking to think he'd wanted to help her. Even back then. But had she been swayed by emotion? Letting herself be influenced by his touch, his kiss, how he made her feel loved?

The shift in their relationship had been something she'd wanted for years. She'd told herself that he was waiting for her to grow up, yet he could be playing her. Her chest kicked with anguish and she pulled in a ragged breath, trying to think objectively.

In Justin's defense, the time line wasn't quite right. He'd kissed her before she questioned his whereabouts about that missing hour. It had been after the kiss that she'd dug into the files and learned she'd been his sole alibi. He hadn't even known about her suspicions until the next day when they drove to the K-9 facility. And he'd seemed truly shocked. Definitely not faking.

It was hard to think and drive safely so she veered onto the next exit and pulled onto the shoulder. Leaning back against the headrest, she stared unseeingly over the dashboard.

Justin cared for her but that didn't mean he wasn't responsible for Erin's disappearance. The two didn't have to be mutually exclusive. She had to accept the possibility that the hands that had held her so tenderly last night may have ended Erin's life.

Then what? Had he dumped her body like garbage and then coolly pretended to help Nikki search all these years? The idea was so ludicrous, it left her shaking her head.

A few cuts on Pancho didn't mean Justin was guilty. Horses kicked and bit each other all the time. Stormy had been a bully and she had the vague recollection that he and Pancho were turned out together. Pancho probably cut himself by rubbing against the fence or rolling on a rock. *And hadn't Justin said the police spoke to other people who'd confirmed his presence at the stable?* But that hadn't been confirmed in her office file.

Steeling herself, she swung her car back onto the road. The cuts could have been made by teeth, not spurs. If they were on both sides, they were probably rider inflicted. But until she saw the actual proof, she wasn't going to agonize over ugly suspicions. Justin deserved her faith.

It took twenty-six minutes to speed to Robert's neighborhood. She parked beneath the shaded oak in front of his house and scrambled from the car. It was still early morning but already the sun was too hot to leave Gunner in the car.

"Come on, fellow," she called, jogging up the walkway and shaking out her keys. She couldn't remember a time when she didn't have a key although it had been years since she'd popped by when Robert wasn't home, despite his insistence she feel free to use the pool.

Gunner loped past her and waited on the upper step, eager for her to unlock the door. No doubt, he was anticipating a juicy dog bone. She wouldn't be here long enough to justify removing one from the freezer but he'd have a few minutes to sniff around the grass. At least her dog was having a good morning: first Justin's yard and now Robert's.

She opened the front door and hurried to the back patio, making sure Gunner trotted past the pool and flowerbeds before sliding the screen door shut. Then she rushed into the kitchen and scanned the counters for the file. Saw nothing.

She walked into the den but the coffee table was empty except for a shiny golf magazine. Then she groaned in realization. Robert had dropped by her office on the way to his golf game. Obviously he had Pancho's summary report in his car. She'd been too impulsive, driving across town for nothing, wasting time and gas.

She trudged back to the patio door and glanced through the screen. Gunner was rolling on the thick grass, eyes closed in bliss. Clearly he didn't think this impromptu stop was a waste. She'd give him a few more minutes before heading to her office.

On the other hand, she didn't want to agonize all day about the location of Pancho's cuts. It would be better to find out where Robert was golfing and simply pick up the file there. He'd have to interrupt his game though and she was loath to bother him. He and his friends were extremely competitive.

She pressed her head against the screen door, accepting she'd have to wait until tonight. At least Robert would have time to dig out the entire file then, and not just a one-page summary.

Or maybe she could find it?

Brightening, she strode into the guest room. She and Erin had often played in the attic and the fold-down staircase was easy to use. She reached up and lowered the stairs, giving it an experimental shake. The steps were rather wobbly but if they held Robert's weight, surely they'd hold hers.

She climbed to the top rung, pulled out her phone and scanned the floor with its light. Her movement stirred up dust, causing her to sneeze five times in quick succession. She swiped at her watering eyes then found a dangling string and turned on the overhead bulb.

She'd never been in the attic without Erin. The space was darker than she remembered and much less cluttered. Cobwebs draped over exposed wooden beams and a hanging sticky tape was dotted with the carcasses of black flies. At one time, the attic had been a treasure trove of toys, pool floats and Christmas decorations. Now there were no toys, only cardboard boxes set in a row. It shouldn't take long to find the information.

Robert didn't appear to have taken many files into retirement, probably only Erin's. Hopefully, the contents were labeled.

She pulled herself up and kneeled beside the first box. Nothing was written on the outside so she raised the top and peered beneath the lid. Her jaw dropped when she saw the contents.

CHAPTER TWENTY-SIX

NIKKI SANK TO HER KNEES beside the bulging cardboard box, struggling for balance. The box didn't contain files at all, but horse brushes: brand new ones with shiny wooden backs and sparkling clean bristles. There was even a small rounded body brush that would fit in a girl's hand. STORMY, it said on the back.

She remembered printing the pony's name. But the brush had disappeared before she'd ever had a chance to take it to the barn. And she remembered why.

She slipped her hand beneath the leather strap, running a finger through the soft bristles. Robert had often dropped off horse items, aware money was tight and that their mom refused to set foot in a tack shop. But that was around the same time Erin was losing interest in horses, and gaining interest in boys. And her moodiness had escalated.

"Don't buy us such stupid things," Erin had yelled at Robert. "Only idiots bring brushes for horses they don't own."

Robert's face had blanched and Nikki had felt terrible. He wasn't used to seeing Erin so antagonistic.

"I'd love to have my own brush," Nikki had said, trying to make him feel better. "Now I'll be able to straighten Stormy's mane."

She'd picked up a marker, printed the pony's name, and was just about to draw a big heart. But Erin had pulled the marker from Nikki's hand and tugged her from the room. "If you want to buy us something sensible," Erin had called over her shoulder. "Buy us a horse. One that can jump, and good enough that Nikki can take to shows."

Nikki had been horrified at such rudeness. Her sister had turned increasingly volatile but not usually when Robert was visiting. Nikki and her mother tended to take the brunt. Although those last months, the outbursts had escalated. It was bittersweet that Nikki's last image of Erin had been her grateful wave as she rode into the woods...a ride that Nikki had enabled, and from which Erin had never returned.

She swiped at her eyes then pulled more items from the box. This was a treasure trove: from hoof picks and curry combs to horse liniments and organic fly spray. She would have been over the moon to have this stuff. And it didn't end there.

The second box contained even bigger ticket items: fitted riding shirts, luxurious leather belts with dainty buckles, and two pink saddle pads embroidered with their initials. At the very bottom of the box, carefully wrapped in a grooming towel, was a designer riding helmet, just like the ones the older girls wore.

Dust was making her eyes water and she jammed everything back in the boxes. The tack store must have been delighted to see Robert coming. But Erin's disappearance and her mother's subsequent barn ban had prevented the items from ever being used. They were forever wasted, stuck in this depressing attic. Maybe Justin would know of a needy kid who would appreciate Robert's generosity.

And she needed to get back on track and remember why she'd climbed up here.

Subdued, she opened the remaining box and checked inside. But there were no police files, only a collection of vaguely familiar photo albums. She lifted the cover and her mother's smiling face beamed back at her. The rest of the pages were the same, filled with photos of her mother, Robert and her dad. Her mom had banished all pictures of her father from the house, but obviously loyal Robert had kept them safe.

Nikki swiped at her eyes, accepting that it wasn't just the dust that bothered her. And she was so relieved the pictures hadn't been trashed. It would be wonderful to have some photos of her parents, back when everyone was happy. She'd been so young when her father died and she shouldn't have taken his suicide as a personal rejection.

Robert, Justin and even Tony thought she'd been too judgmental. And they'd been right. After all, more than one cop escaped the darkness with a self-inflicted bullet.

She flipped through the remaining albums, feeling herself further soften. Her parents looked so beautiful, beaming with optimism and vitality. Even Robert grinned in a way she'd never seen before.

And then it changed. Her father disappeared from the pictures, taking with him her mom's sparkle. Nikki and Erin still seemed to be having fun though, splashing in Robert's pool and spraying him with water. Erin was the spitting image of their mother, blond hair plastering her face, while Nikki looked more like her dad. But this time her nose didn't curl at that admission.

She slowed, turning each page more deliberately now, completely engrossed. Her childhood was contained in these albums and clearly it hadn't all been bad. There were even photos of her and Erin, dressed in clumsy rubber boots and jeans, their very first day working at the stable. Robert had driven them their entire first week, worried the school bus wouldn't get them there on time. There were even pictures of Stormy and a few other horses, including one of Erin jumping a cross rail.

She scanned the pictures, noting how Erin's work pants changed from faded jeans to form-fitting white breeches. And how her smile turned as artificial as her clothes. In her tight clothing and fancy riding helmet, she resembled the stuck-up boarders she'd been so determined to copy.

Erin's eyes looked darker too and it wasn't only the result of makeup. She had a defiant look that Nikki didn't remember seeing. If Erin had looked at Justin with such insolence, it was a wonder she hadn't been fired on the spot.

Then there were no more pictures, only empty pages in a sad unfinished album.

Nikki replaced the lid on the box, washed by a myriad of feelings. She was grateful Robert had kept the pictures and she'd like to have her own copies. He must have been saving the photos, along with all the horse items, waiting until she was emotionally ready. The clothes and helmet were no longer of use but she'd always treasure Stormy's brush.

Something nagged at her but the thought was fleeting, dissolving before it could fully form. And she must have misunderstood Robert because there were certainly no case files here. Definitely nothing about Pancho.

She sent him a text even though he was probably on the golf course by now and wouldn't answer until the afternoon. *Where's the full report on Erin's horse?*

His quick answer surprised her. *Attic.*

I'm at your place now and don't see it. She paused on the ladder to finish the text. *Lots of pictures though. Fun looking through the albums.*

She slipped the phone in her pocket and reached up to shove the staircase back into place. Her phone chirped and she answered without checking the screen, assuming it was Robert.

"Did you figure out the coffee maker?" Justin asked. "Just wonder if you want me to come back. And help you with anything."

His voice was low and intimate, stirring vivid memories from last night. Heat warmed her face. And every feminine part. She couldn't help thinking about all the delightful ways he could help.

"I already left your place," she said, shaken by her rush of desire. It didn't seem fair to indulge in sexual fantasies while searching for a potentially incriminating report. "I'm at Robert's now."

"Regrettable."

"Yes," she breathed, then squeezed her lips tight, shocked by the longing that spilled from her voice.

"Dammit, I love it when you talk dirty."

"It's one word." She smiled in spite of herself, amazed at how light he made her feel.

"But it's all I need to hear," he said. "Did Gunner have fun chasing the squirrels?"

"Yes, he did... How did you know about the squirrel?"

"Video."

Her hand tightened around the ladder. She'd noticed the cameras outside Justin's house. No doubt he also had surveillance inside, just better concealed.

"You were watching us?" She didn't hide her indignation but at the same time she was relieved she hadn't snooped in his office.

"No, Nikki," he said gently. "I turn off the interior when I'm home. Or when there's no risk."

"But you were gone. I was there alone."

"That's right," he said.

The fact that he trusted her made her feel warm again. As well as slightly guilty. "I did go in your office," she said. "But I was looking for a pen. I didn't open any drawers or look for anything."

"Erin's files aren't there," he said. "And your sister's case has been officially re-opened. If you want any information, you only have to ask."

The idea that she could ask, and receive, timely information—without Robert pleading for favors from old cop friends—was difficult to grasp. Of course, she was a licensed investigator now. Not a young girl. "Is it your case?" she asked.

"No, it's been assigned to one of our cold case experts. His name is Philip Lenco. His office is just down the hall from mine."

She should have been relieved Justin wasn't in charge, especially when her concerns seem to resurface with every new piece of information. It was probably not possible to see the police report on Pancho. But this was a good way to test him. "You're saying I can be privy to any information from Erin's case?"

She braced herself for a refusal, or at least a lengthy explanation about redaction, but his answer surprised her.

"Of course," he said.

"Great," she said quickly. "Then can you tell me about the detective's report on Pancho?"

"There's isn't much. There were some sweat stains beneath Pancho's saddle indicating mild exertion before being tied to that tree. Nothing noteworthy."

"No cuts?"

"Just that old abrasion on his hock where he scraped the stall. We were treating it with an antiseptic. Remember?"

She nodded even though he couldn't see her. "Yes, we used a blue cream that the student vet left," she said. "You said it would keep the flies away."

"It works too. I still use that stuff." His voice turned serious. "Let me know when you want to come by. You can't make a copy but you can read the full report in my office."

"Wait." She rubbed her forehead. Something didn't fit. He'd just claimed there were no spur marks—yet he'd agreed to let her read the official report. "What about Pancho's other cuts? What did we rub on those? You know...the cuts on his sides?"

Justin turned silent. A chair squeaked and he told someone to wait a moment. A door closed. Moments later, he spoke again. "Pancho had no other cuts," he said. "And it's not like you to beat around the bush. What are you really asking, Nik?"

She stiffened, bracing her shoulder against the stairs. He was too smart. She should have known he'd see through her questions.

"If you're asking about rider-inflicted marks," Justin went on, "there weren't any. And exactly where was that trail leading you?"

"Erin could be hard on a horse when she was upset," Nikki said. "Maybe she spurred Pancho, trying to get him to jump the brook. You know, to keep up with the other girls."

"You believe that's what made her dismount and walk away? That's your theory? That she didn't want to ride a bloody horse back to the barn and face the consequences?"

Nikki didn't speak for a moment, knowing her next words would cause irreparable harm. She straightened, crossing her arms, hating how she felt so defensive and wishing she could just let it go. *But Erin was her sister.*

And her words came out brittle as shards of glass and just as painful. "Or maybe she faced the consequences in the woods," she said.

She heard his sharp intake of breath, then a low curse. "Dammit, Nikki. Is your opinion of me really that low?"

Her chest squeezed but she was unable to back down. "You and Robert are always talking about staying objective. To be tenacious and follow the evidence."

"But it's as if you want me to be guilty. Are you so afraid of your feelings that you're fabricating evidence?"

"I'm not fabricating. It's right here!" Her voice rose and she gestured so quickly her hand hit the ladder. "And my feelings for you have nothing to do with the facts."

"So that's why you dropped by my house last night. So you could search my office. Seems you're still willing to go to great lengths for your sister. I certainly hope the pleasure you gave me last night wasn't too big a sacrifice." His laugh was rough and devoid of humor.

"No. I care for you." But even to her, the protest sounded weak. And now she wished he had turned the surveillance on, so she could prove she hadn't been snooping. "I wasn't looking for files, not last night. But now I am and I just want to reconcile everything. I'm just asking you to look at this report and explain."

But she was talking to blank air. Because Justin had ended the call.

CHAPTER TWENTY-SEVEN

NIKKI SLUMPED ON A chair in Robert's kitchen, still gripping her phone. If she were Justin, she probably would have hung up too. But she wasn't fabricating evidence. He didn't realize Robert still had contacts inside the police department.

She stared glumly through the screen door. At least Gunner was having fun, sniffing around the flowerbed, his tail swinging. Best to call him inside before he began to dig. It was time to leave anyway. The meeting with Mrs. Carlton was at one o'clock and she still needed to stop by the office.

But her tangled emotions kept her rooted to the chair.

She didn't want Justin to be guilty. But the timeline, his weak shavings alibi, Pancho's cuts. Those facts couldn't be denied. They kept adding up, pointing toward him. It was tempting to gather the reports, drop them on his desk and demand that he explain. He couldn't brush her off then. She had Robert's old files from her office. But she still needed to find the written report on Pancho.

She grabbed her phone and started another text just as the side door to the garage clicked open and Robert strolled in.

"I was just texting you," she said. "You're back early. Is everything okay?"

"Absolutely," Robert said. "But it sounded like you were eager to see that report."

She gave a grateful nod. "Yes. I checked the attic. Then realized it's probably in your car."

Robert glanced through the screen door at Gunner who was sitting in front of the flowerbed, his dark coat outlined by a colorful backdrop of flowers.

"Sorry," she said quickly. "I'll bring him inside."

"He's okay," Robert said. "Just relax. I'll find him a bone, make us some tea and you can tell me why this horse report is so important."

"What about your golf?"

"It's not as important as helping you." He plugged the kettle in and shot her a quizzical smile. "I rescheduled and came home. So, what's bothering you?"

"It's probably nothing," she said, feeling protective of Justin. But she needed to talk this over and Robert was always an excellent sounding board. She had his full attention too—his expression was intent.

She blew out a conflicted sigh. "Erin was caught once forcing Pancho over some jumps. Being too aggressive with her spurs. Obviously Justin didn't like it. Nobody did. So I wondered, you know, if maybe that's what happened at the brook. If she was hurting the horse and..." It was hard to say anything more so she just swallowed, letting her voice trail off.

"So, it was Justin?" Robert's eyes widened. "You think he was upset at how Erin treated the horse? So he killed her? Then hid her body?"

Nikki rubbed her temple. Robert's words were so blunt, the idea seemed ludicrous. She gave her head a shake. "No," she said. "I don't think that. And even if something happened through some freak accident, he wouldn't have hidden her body. He just wouldn't do that."

She sagged in her chair, flooded with relief. She'd been so focused on small pieces, sometimes she couldn't see the bigger picture.

"Justin wouldn't do something like that," she repeated. "He respects life too much. He even had a special place for burying the cats. And it doesn't matter about his alibi or Pancho's cuts. He would have carried Erin out of the woods. He would have brought her back to us and faced the consequences. That's just who he is."

"So we're back to square one." Robert pulled two mugs from the cupboard. "Guess it's time to let this whole thing go. Move on."

"No, the case has been reopened. Carlton wasn't a suspect before. And this time we won't be shut out, not with Justin around. They'll listen to our ideas. Every one of them."

Robert unplugged the screaming kettle, his back to her. "You two are close again?"

They'd certainly been close last night, she thought, relieved Robert was busy making tea. She made an agreeable sound deep in her throat, relieved she wasn't prone to blushing.

"A cold case expert has been assigned to the case," she said. "New eyes. New perspective. And Justin promised they'll look at all the information we've gathered over the years. Review everyone's memories."

"Good, because you have a lot to offer. Although a kid's memory can be spotty."

"Yes, but the stuff in the attic will help. I didn't realize you'd kept all those pictures. Glad you did though. The new investigator will be able to get a better sense of Erin."

"I thought you'd want those albums some day," Robert said. "Did you have time to look in all the boxes?"

"Sure did. You were so supportive of us. Shirts, breeches, helmet. And they weren't cheap brands."

She beamed him a grateful smile, watching as he fumbled in a cupboard drawer. "While you're making tea," she added, "I'll go out to the garage and grab the report on Pancho."

"Wait, Nikki. There's no rush." A spoon clinked and he walked over to the table, balancing two cups of tea.

There actually was a rush. But he didn't understand her urgency, the need to show the report to Justin and give him a chance to explain. There had to be a reason for the conflicting reports about Pancho's cuts. She shot a wistful look at the garage door then sipped her tea, relieved it wasn't too hot.

"What time is your appointment with Mrs. Carlton?" Robert asked, obviously picking up on her impatience but unaware of the reason.

"One o'clock. But I need to read that report on Pancho first and see who signed it. There has to be a mistake. Justin said Erin's horse had no injuries."

"You trust him?" Robert's voice sharpened. "In spite of everything? In spite of what your mother thought?"

"Mom wasn't right about a lot of things," Nikki said. "She was never emotionally healthy. And the more I think about it, the more it's obvious Justin couldn't be involved. Even if he hurt Erin by accident, he never would have dumped her body. He's too decent, too respectful for that."

"But what if they were having sex? That would justify concealing a body. His life would have been ruined."

"He's not like that." Nikki took another sip of tea, remembering Justin's horror when she accused him of liking Erin. "He was always professional around us."

"Maybe with you," Robert said. "But Erin was older, more appealing."

Nikki winced. She'd accepted that her mother had loved Erin more. But she remembered Robert as being more fair with his attention. Admittedly the gifts and excursions had been geared toward Erin but at least he'd always bought two of everything—unless the items were wildly expensive, like the Apple watch and music system.

But then Erin had switched her interest to horses and life had been wonderful. Her mother's coolness hadn't hurt nearly as much when Nikki had a pony to hug.

She sipped her warm tea, comforted by the cup in her hands. This was an uncomfortable subject but she felt more accepting now. Ready to hear the truth. "Why did Mom love Erin more than me?"

"Because you reminded her too much of Paul." Robert answered without a moment's hesitation. "And he broke her heart. She loved that man until the day she died."

"I wish she hadn't," Nikki said.

Robert sighed. "Yes, but your father was handsome, smart and exciting. Women always fell over him, even though he didn't give a damn. You're too much like him, a feminine clone."

"You make it sound like that's a bad thing."

"It is." Robert steepled his fingers, not touching his tea. "Looking at you, seeing him, just reminds me how he took everything I ever wanted."

Nikki blinked, shocked by his harsh honesty. At least she thought she blinked. Her eyelids felt heavy.

"Don't look so surprised," Robert said. "I dated her first. She was mine. Do you know how hard it was to pretend I didn't care? To give the wedding toast, to see her swell with another man's spawn, to babysit you when they went away?"

"B-but you were his best friend."

Robert snorted. "He got everything. The woman, the job, the accolades."

"And a very short life," Nikki said, not liking this side of Robert. Jealousy didn't flatter anyone. She'd come back tomorrow when he was more balanced.

She glanced out the screen door at Gunner. He had dirt over his front legs, and this was a bad time for him to be digging. Or for drawing attention to the fact that he'd buried a bone in the flowerbeds.

She shot a wary look across the table, hoping Robert wouldn't notice. Fortunately Robert wasn't looking outside. His eyes were riveted on her face.

"Your father did have a short life," he said. "Everything was better after that. But I thought she'd turn to me. Instead I had to be satisfied with leftovers."

Nikki's head pounded. Not only was Robert talking oddly but his eyes were weird. Like a stranger's, cold, hard and full of venom.

"I didn't want it like this," he went on. "I thought it was over. You shouldn't have gone poking in the attic."

"W-what?" She struggled to follow his reasoning, to push the words through her thick lips. Both her mouth and brain felt clumsy.

Robert leaned back in his chair, studying her as if she were an insect beneath a microscope. "How are you feeling, my dear? I have great respect for your martial arts skills—I've seen your workouts. But you look suitably sluggish."

"What?" she repeated, grabbing the ends of the table, struggling to stay erect.

"I tried to stop you and Justin from getting close," Robert said. "Didn't want the case reopened. But you'll never give up and Justin's too good. Although if you hadn't seen Erin's helmet, you might have remained an acceptable risk.

"She wanted to talk that day," Robert went on. "Told me to meet her by the bridge. But she was in a strange mood, talking about some school boy she liked, saying I had to stay away. Too upset to be reasonable. About anything." Robert's voice thickened. "She threatened to tell. I couldn't let her do that. Your mother meant everything to me."

Nikki's brain felt molasses slow. She heard Robert's words but they were too slimy to grasp. "Tell?" she croaked.

"Come on. You have to understand. It wasn't my fault. Erin was a beautiful girl. And very precocious." He shrugged and raised his palms. "She looked like your mom. So I took what I could get."

The blood drained from Nikki's face. "You sicko!"

She lurched forward but her legs felt detached from her body. She slid sideways. Would have fallen if Robert hadn't shoved her back onto the chair.

"You're always so feisty," he said, propping her up. "But you're in no condition to be calling me names. Besides, it was your fault Erin didn't want me around. She kept warning me not to touch you, as if I'd want any female who reminded me of Paul." He gave a dismissive snort. "She wanted to phone you after our talk. To ask you to meet her where she'd tied that stupid horse. But at that point she was yelling threats. I really had no choice but to drive her back here. Take care of things."

Nikki gaped. Robert looked like a stranger, an evil caricature of a man she'd always thought of as an uncle. Her stunned gaze dropped to the tea. He must have laced it with something. And he'd been watching her so closely, gauging her reaction. How much worse was she going to get? How much time did she have?

"Another couple hours," Robert said. "Your death will be after your supposed meeting with Carlton's wife."

I'm thinking out loud. Her chest kicked with panic as she realized she was in worse shape than she'd thought. Robert's face was pulsing now, his mouth moving like a slow-motion puppet. It was weird and horrifying all at the same time. And it was becoming increasingly difficult to absorb his words. She widened her fingers over her thigh, frantically pinching her skin, hoping the pain would kick-start her stalling brain.

"Carlton is still protective of his wife," Robert was saying. "So everything will lead to him. And I'll be able to keep Erin's helmet. You're the only one who would remember she was wearing it. And possibly Justin."

Nikki's lips felt thick but she knew she was grimacing. The helmet, of course. All the girls had looked so stylish that day. And Erin had been wearing a matching helmet, the same one that was up in the attic.

"Is that why you're doing this?" she tried to ask but her words came out slurred.

"I didn't want to," Robert said. "But once you saw that helmet it was only a matter of time before you remembered. And no matter how many reports I planted, you kept getting closer to Justin, spurring each other on. And now they're re-opening the case." He spat so aggressively, spittle flew across the table. "I can't have detectives digging through the pictures, seeing me with your mother, questioning my statement that *he* was suicidal. I wanted to leave a note but couldn't quite copy his writing."

Nikki's heartbeat thrashed in her ears as she stared at the stranger sitting across the table. "You? You did it? You sh-shot Dad?"

"Of course, but it didn't help. She still didn't want me. At least I didn't have to see them together. Besides, for a while I had sweet Erin."

Nikki wanted to plug her ears, to shut him out, but most of all she wanted to leap across the table and wrap her hands around his throat. Erin's erratic behavior, the shadows in her beautiful eyes, had been created by this man. Sonja's warning and the ominous picture on the tarot card flashed through her head.

"*You're* the devil," she breathed.

CHAPTER TWENTY-EIGHT

"I'M NOT SURE IF I'M the devil," Robert chided. "I invested a lot of time in your family. Only fair I receive something in return."

Nikki gaped. Even his features looked different now. His mouth thinner, his eyes ugly. And though he had no horns, he really was the devil, taking everyone she'd ever loved. His sly digs about Justin, even his pretend defense of her father, had all been contrived. And she'd listened, trusting him, letting him shape her beliefs even after he planted fake evidence in her office. And in her head.

"Don't look at me like that," Robert chided. "I'm just a man who fell in love with the wrong woman. If you had given up like any normal person, this wouldn't have to happen. But you always wanted to be with your sister. Now I'm granting your wish."

His gaze slid outside to Gunner who was still sitting by the flowerbed. Eagerly waiting. Wagging his tail, exactly the way he had at the riding stable.

Comprehension struck, along with Nikki's horrified gasp. Erin was buried in those flowerbeds. That was why Robert had been so disturbed whenever Gunner sniffed around the flowers. And the reason he'd gone to so much effort fencing in a separate dog area. It also explained why Gunner's interest had never waned, even when Robert served him unlimited dog bones.

She gave an agonized moan. All this time, wondering, hoping, searching. Her mother had died not knowing what happened to her beloved daughter. They'd thought Robert was their savior when all along he'd been a vicious murderer.

"You fucking monster."

But her words were weak, slurred with helpless fury, and Robert only grinned. "I'm the same man I was yesterday. And I've taken enough insults from you girls. Now I just need to tie up some loose ends."

He rose, strode to the freezer and pulled out a brown-wrapped package. He slid open the screen door before she realized it was a bone for Gunner. *Poison?*

"Leave it, Gunner," she called. But her voice was too weak and Gunner was too far away to hear.

Robert strode across the concrete deck, waving the bone in his hand. He whipped back his arm and tossed the bone high over the pool. "Get it, Gunner!" he called, his voice excited.

Gunner obediently wheeled away from the flowers, charged across the concrete deck and launched himself high in the air. Water sprayed as he splashed in the middle of the pool and wrapped his jaws around the bone. He turned, triumphant, swimming a half circle as he searched for a place to climb out.

However, the pool was too deep, the sides too high, and he looked up at Robert, his eyes a question.

"No," she moaned. *Gunner will drown!* Her arms flailed around the table as she struggled to rise. Robert stepped inside, pulled the screen shut and roughly shoved her back in the chair.

"Well, that's taken care of." He rubbed his hands together. "Gunner's a big strong dog. How long do you suppose he'll last?"

"D-don't," she said. "Not necessary."

"It certainly is. His digging was worrisome, the way he always sat by the yellow marigolds, as if he knew. Well, that's no longer a problem."

She wanted to close her eyes and banish the nightmare. To wake up to a new day and the Robert she thought she'd known, a man who fenced his yard and supplied bones because he cared for them, not because it was the best way to keep Gunner distracted.

And now he was making her sit and watch her dog drown.

A sob clogged her throat. Gunner wasn't even worried yet. He swam large circles around the pool, water rippling in his wake, the bone gripped beneath his strong jaws. Every few seconds, he glanced toward the door, as if wondering when she'd show up. He didn't bark or make a sound. Maybe he thought he'd be scolded for jumping in the pool, something that was always a no-no, simply because it was a death trap.

Tears blurred her eyes. She didn't want to watch but couldn't look away. The shallow end was too deep for him to touch the bottom, the pool deck too high to let him hook his paws. And he wouldn't go near the vertical ladder. Even now, he gave it a wide berth, viewing it as an instrument of torture, something that gave a painful shock when his paws touched the rungs. As Tony had said, Gunner wouldn't climb a ladder to save his life.

"Please." A sob built in her throat. "Help him. You don't have to do this. He can't say anything."

Robert raised an eyebrow. "Interesting you'd beg for your dog's life but not yours. But the answer is no. Because he tries to tell, every time he's here. Besides, everyone knows you two are always together. He has to disappear."

"Gunner, up!" She tried to motion with her hand even though her frantic voice was too weak to carry. But her arm flopped over the table, resembling a beached fish rather than a firm signal.

"He can't get out," Robert said smugly. "We all know ladders are his weakness. And he trusts me. Dumb dog doesn't have a clue what's happening."

That was the horrible truth. Gunner knew Robert, viewed him as a provider. He'd never even heard Robert yell. And her motor skills were too impaired, her voice too weak to alert Gunner to danger. But he had to try to climb out of the pool now, before he was too exhausted.

She tried calling again, her mouth working ineffectually even as tears warmed her face. She was vaguely conscious of Robert leaving the room.

Steps sounded. Robert towered above her as he dropped her phone and car keys on the table. "I moved your car into the garage. Once it's dark, I'll dump it out by Carlton's estate. But don't worry. You and Gunner will be staying right here."

She hadn't realized Robert had left the room long enough to move her car. He seemed to have everything planned, as if he knew it would come to this. Now he was dumping the contents of a plastic bottle into the sink, humming tunelessly. Oh, God. A homemade silencer.

She peered frantically at Gunner. He was still swimming, but kept twisting his head toward the door. As if he realized this wasn't normal.

She had to give him some sign, a signal that he needed to try to save himself. But it would take something extreme.

"You'll like being together," Robert said, cheerfully placing the bottle beside her gun and phone. "Now is there anything else we should discuss? I can't hold a funeral for you, at least not immediately. But everyone will assume you're dead, and that Carlton was responsible. He may even be credited with all three murders although personally I'd prefer that your father remain a suicide."

Robert's face was hazy and it was difficult to process his words. Her head felt like it was floating, separate from her body. Clearly though, her father was Robert's hot spot. And she had to hurry before she ran out of time. She no longer had enough coordination to pinch her hand so she jabbed her finger backward against the table, welcoming the spike of pain. Something, anything, to keep her words coherent.

"Dad...was...better cop than you," she said. "Better m-man."

Robert's eyes slitted.

Her next words came out even clearer. "Mom said...better lover too."

"Shut up!"

She smiled although her mouth was too numb to feel her lips, so maybe she didn't smile at all. But she was able to force a snicker. "S-said...you sucked."

Robert stalked around the table. "Shut up. Now!"

"Dad's friends... Everyone knew...you could never satisfy a grown woman—"

The blow came so fast she didn't see Robert's fist. It knocked her off the chair, smashing her head against the base of the counter. Her vision spotted and something warm trickled from her nose. She prayed it was blood. Hoped he wouldn't be able to clean it up.

And she fervently hoped Gunner would notice the violence and be motivated enough to climb the ladder. If he was spooked enough, he might be able to escape.

The toe of Robert's white golf shoe was inches from her nose, marked now with blood spatter. Investigators would have something, if only they knew where to look.

She swallowed the metallic taste and forced her head off the tile, trying to bring him into focus. She had to keep him off balance, hope he made another mistake. His voice wasn't loud enough to alert neighbors but Gunner must be shocked to hear Robert yelling. And if she could just get close enough to scratch his face, surely someone would ask questions.

"That's why you had to rape a fifteen-year-old," she went on. "Not enough of a man. Not like Dad."

"Shut up!" Robert was still hollering, his face mottled with rage. "That bitch never appreciated me. None of your fucking family did." The kick to her face was so vicious, her next words turned into a choke of pain.

Robert barged around the table, cursing and reaching for the gun. Last chance. She had to push herself up, try to scratch him. But her arms felt weighted down, her fingers barely able to curl into fists.

Her brain and body seemed to be misfiring and an odd mixture of wet heat needled her skin. Something clattered to the floor. Her ears hurt. And Robert was making strange noises, no longer swearing but making coarse animal sounds.

She pressed her cheek against the tile. Trying to turn. To see. But the only thing in her blurred sight was a green pop bottle. Then she recognized Robert's bloody shoes. He was pressed against the counter, only ten feet away. And he clutched a dripping dog, one arm wrapped around Gunner's back, the other waving a gun.

She sobbed. Part relief, part terror. Somehow Gunner had come to her rescue but he was confused. He wasn't attacking like the K-9s at the training center. Wasn't grabbing Robert's gun hand. He knew Robert too well, didn't want to hurt someone who always fed him.

Robert seemed to be moving in slow motion. But he was able to bring the gun around. Able to point it at Gunner's head.

"Fass!" she yelled, pouring all her energy into a desperate holler. Never had she used the German word before but it had been on Gunner's list of commands. Justin had said to only use it when she didn't care if he hurt someone. She certainly didn't care about Robert. She only wanted to stop him from shooting her dog.

Too late! The gun went off. Gunner yelped. Then his jaws clamped around Robert's gun arm. Bones crunched.

"Get him off," Robert screamed.

She ignored him. Could only stare in horror at Gunner's bloody shoulder. He couldn't be hurt too bad. Not judging by his ferocious growls or the vice-like clamp he had on Robert's gun arm. But even as she watched, blood pooled on the floor.

"Good dog," she managed, curling on her side. She drew her legs up and inched forward, desperately scanning the floor for the gun. But it was way over by the fridge. An impossible distance. At least Robert couldn't reach it either. But Gunner couldn't hold him forever, and her dog needed medical help.

Her phone was closer, lying on the floor just beyond the plastic bottle. Four feet seemed an impossible distance but she forced herself to crawl, slowly, laboriously, fighting her fuzziness. Her gaze met Robert's, his expression shifting from pain to predatory cunning.

"You're going to pass out soon," he said softly, taking care not to further excite Gunner. The dog was still growling, his jaws locked around Robert's arm, pinning him in place but not causing any more damage.

"If you call the police," Robert said, "they'll shoot Gunner. He isn't going to let any stranger get close. So if you want him to live, you'd better calm him down first."

Nikki ignored him. Obviously he was hoping she'd pass out before she could call 911. Even now, waves of gray blurred her vision. She bit her lip, concentrating on moving her right leg, then her left in a clumsy crawling motion, focusing on the length of beige tile that separated her outstretched hand from the phone.

She didn't want to hear Robert's voice, didn't want to see his satisfaction, and she certainly didn't want to see her dog's shattered shoulder. How long could Gunner hold him?

Definitely longer than she'd be conscious. But if the police burst in, Robert was correct. Gunner would try to protect her. They'd have to shoot.

She wanted to tell Gunner to rip out Robert's throat. That would solve one problem. But it wouldn't help her dog. He'd be in full protective mode then, attacking anyone who tried to get close. Police and paramedics wouldn't understand, wouldn't realize he'd only been following her command. Under the circumstances, they'd pull their guns. Injured humans always came first.

It was hard to think, to weigh the options. Her brain, usually so quick, had quit working. Robert was still talking, trying to confuse her, using up the last seconds before she passed out. His voice turned more triumphant as he watched her fade.

She couldn't let him win. Couldn't risk Gunner being shot. There was only one man her dog trusted. She just hoped he'd answer.

She crawled the last remaining inch. Forced her hand around the phone. And called Justin.

CHAPTER TWENTY-NINE

NIKKI'S HEAD POUNDED and cotton seemed to clog every corner of her mouth. She pushed her head against the pillow, struggling to swallow. Someone pressed a straw between her lips.

"Little sips," a deep and familiar voice said.

Justin. Memories crashed over her in waves and she jerked forward, her gaze scrabbling around the room. But she didn't see Gunner. Only the cold confines of a hospital room with its tiled floor and pervasive smell of disinfectant. "Gunner?" she croaked.

"With the vet."

She pressed her lips together, wanting to hear more but afraid to ask. Judging by the gentle way Justin held her hand and the dark hollows shadowing his eyes, he had bad news.

"How bad is he?" she finally asked. "Did the police hurt him?"

Justin shook his head. But he leaned over the bed, staring at her with a haunted expression.

"Is Gunner going to be okay?" she asked. "Will he live?" She kept her eyes on Justin's face, desperate for reassurance. He always told the truth, always kept his promises. So if she could only get him to say the words, Gunner would live.

"He'll live. They removed a bullet from his shoulder and he'll need extensive rehab. But Tony has offered full use of the center's facilities and that will go a long way in regaining mobility."

Such relief swept her, it was hard to concentrate as Justin went on to speak about blood loss and ligaments and a therapeutic swimming pool. All she could do was grip his hand in gratitude. Her last conscious fear had been that the police would shoot Gunner, unaware that he was a hero. The dog who wouldn't climb a ladder to save his life had finally done it—to save hers.

"When I got your call," Justin said, "I could hear him growling. That's when I knew it was Robert." He shook his head, his eyes ravaged. "They'd looked at him way back but never considered him a likely suspect."

"So you know what he did?" She couldn't remember what she'd said on the call to Justin, only that it had been difficult to form the words. "Did you get to his house first?"

"No, I was five minutes behind emergency responders. But I advised there was a K-9 in the home and requested they wait for me if possible. So they ignored Robert's insistence that Gunner was vicious and needed to be shot. Amazingly, you were still conscious, still trying to stop anyone from hurting him. You weren't very coherent though, just stubborn and full of fight." A smile softened the corners of his mouth before he quickly sobered. "It was the evidence techs who found the spot where Gunner had been digging. They did recover remains. I'm sorry, but it's probably Erin."

"It is." Nikki shifted, lifting her head from the pillow and leaning against Justin's comforting arm. "I found her helmet in the attic. The one she'd been wearing that day. That's why Robert decided I was a threat." Her voice stalled as she remembered his utter ruthlessness. It took a moment to continue.

"He put something in my tea," she went on. "Then he threw a bone, luring Gunner into the pool. I never realized he hated me so much."

She squeezed her eyes shut. Many of the details were fuzzy but the virulence on Robert's face was seared into her brain. And that was one of the most painful things to absorb. She was vaguely aware of Justin assuring her she didn't have any broken bones, that they were just waiting on blood tests in order to determine the drug Robert had used.

She tried to listen. But she was numb, unable to reconcile the murderous Robert with the caring man she'd loved. And too gutted to ask any more questions. She could feel Justin watching, sensed his concern, but she just wanted to sleep. And not think or talk or feel.

"Robert certainly underestimated Gunner," Justin said. "There's a huge rip where the dog tore through the screen. Gunner finally had enough motivation to climb a ladder. Naturally the K-9 unit is demanding his return."

Her eyes opened and she jackknifed forward, all numbness pushed aside by the idea of losing Gunner. "No way! I'll fight any ownership claim. Do you still have a receipt? Anything like that?" Her hand fisted around Justin's fingers. It was then she caught his relieved smile.

"That's my girl," he said, and it was obvious he realized that her entire foundation had been rocked. She'd blamed her father for wrecking their family when it had been Robert, her father's trusted friend. And Justin didn't even know the worst.

"There's more." She sucked in an achy breath. "Robert killed my father. Set it up to look like a suicide."

The teasing glint disappeared from Justin's face. His arm tightened around her shoulders and somehow his shock made it easier for her to sit straighter and keep talking. "It was jealousy over Mom. Robert kept pictures in his attic. They used to date. That's why Robert chose Erin as her stand-in. He was having sex with my sister and she threatened to tell."

Justin's gentle touch didn't change but his jaw turned granite hard. "You need to talk to the detectives," he said. "As soon as you're able."

"So you're not here in that capacity?"

"No."

She thought for a moment then tucked her head back into his shoulder. She felt too fragile to talk to anyone else right now. Her brain kept skipping back to fragmented memories when Erin had tugged her away from Robert. She'd thought her sister wanted all the attention when really Erin had been trying to protect her. And the more Nikki remembered, the more her guilt swelled.

"I never understood Erin," she said brokenly. "Never guessed..."

"Of course you didn't. Neither did your mother. Or me." There was a pensive note to Justin's voice and she knew he was remembering all the times Robert had visited the barn and watched them ride.

She pressed her head against the pillow, her chest feeling as if it was about to cave in. For years she'd been driven by the idea of finding Erin, alive and well. It had been Robert who'd helped her become a certified investigator. Robert who had paid for all the extra martial arts lessons. "Just in case you ever meet up with Erin's abductor," he had said. And all along he'd been the snake in the grass.

"Where is he now?" she asked.

Justin didn't pretend not to understand. "In custody. He was treated for dog bites. He could have been hurt a lot worse...Gunner could have killed him."

She stared at the white sheet covering her feet. Yes, Robert could have been hurt far worse. Perhaps he should have been. She resisted the urge to cross her arms, trying not to second guess her decision.

"I'm surprised you didn't let Gunner finish the job," Justin said, his fingers linking through hers as if in solidarity.

"I wanted to. But the police would have shot him if they found Robert with a ripped-out throat. And Gunner was already hurt. I didn't want him to lose any more blood and possibly die because of a scumball molester."

"Excellent reasons. But when they question you, don't be so honest. Just say you and your dog are trained not to use unnecessary force. Can you do that?"

"A decorated detective shouldn't be encouraging me to lie." However, his support made her feel much less alone. Justin had been at the barn the day Erin disappeared. Their shared guilt had been a large part of what had kept them connected. It had also been a large part of what kept them apart. And Robert's lies and innuendoes, his fake evidence, hadn't helped.

"I'm sorry," she said.

"For what?"

"For trusting Robert more."

"Your guilt left you susceptible," Justin said. "Misplaced though it was. And Robert was smart. He knew how to manipulate your mom into stoking it."

She nodded. Everything Justin said was true but the words didn't make her feel much better. Because she'd sent Erin on that trail ride. She'd put her sister in a position to be alone with a monster. And nothing could be done to change that. Because she knew the harsh truth now... Erin was never coming back.

CHAPTER THIRTY

"WHEN YOU GO BACK TO the vet clinic tonight," Sonja said, "take these treats to Gunner." She reached across her selection of teas and candles and picked up a big box of gourmet dog biscuits. "They'll boost his spirits."

Nikki didn't remember saying Gunner was depressed but she was past questioning Sonja's psychic abilities. And naturally her dog was depressed. He'd been at the clinic for eight days, ever since their encounter with Robert, and his movement was severely restricted. When he left there, it would be months of physio at the K-9 center and though she was beyond grateful for Tony's support, she missed her dog. And he missed her.

"Is there anything else he wants?" Nikki asked humbly. "Besides being able to run again."

Sonja's eyebrows pursed in thought. "A pony," she said.

Nikki laughed but the smile slipped off her face at her friend's serious expression. "You're kidding," Nikki said. "My yard is barely big enough for a dog."

"You can keep it at my place," Sonja said. "All I know is I'm seeing a pony." She turned quiet again, obviously back in her psychic bubble. "And apples," she added. "Erin wants apples."

Nikki froze. It seemed as if her lungs had shrunk and she couldn't get enough air. This was the first occasion since the time Sonja had warned about concrete that she'd brought up Erin's name in a psychic context. And it gutted Nikki knowing that for years her sister had been buried in Robert's yard while she'd sat twenty feet away, smiling and laughing with the man who'd put her there.

She knew the truth now: Knowing someone was dead was far worse than fearing it. And if Erin wanted apples, she would get them, even if Nikki wasn't sure where to take the fruit. Her sister's remains were still at the coroner's although eventually she'd be cremated and placed in the family plot beside their mother and father.

"Maybe she'd like a memorial tree planted somewhere," Nikki said, her mind racing over possible locations.

"No," Sonja said. "The apples are for you. Erin just wants you to be happy. To do things for yourself, not her. Things that make you feel good."

Nikki pressed her ramrod spine back against the chair. She didn't know how apples would make her feel better. Even her work had lost appeal. In fact, she'd just forwarded photos to an insurance company showing their client carrying a bulky sofa. In one of the pictures he'd been grimacing, although she knew that wouldn't soften the insurance company's stance. The fact that he might be cut off from his benefits because he'd been helping his elderly mom didn't leave her feeling very good.

Not much did anymore. Except Justin.

Sonja must have seen the distaste in Nikki's face. "Why don't you stop surveillance work for a while? Go live with your hot detective. Figure out what you want to do now that the mission to find your sister is over. I bet Justin wouldn't mind having you and Gunner around."

Maybe not. But while Nikki seemed to have lost her purpose, Justin was still a driven detective, already immersed in his next case. He'd kissed her goodbye yesterday, reluctant to leave the bed. Yet he'd scooped up his badge and holster with a hunter's enthusiasm. She didn't want to dull that passion by turning needy, always checking the time and wondering when he'd return.

"Just figure out what makes you happy," Sonja continued, "now that you're not obsessed with finding Erin."

Nikki didn't like the word "obsessed." It conjured up images of raging maniacs. And she couldn't just switch off her thoughts. Erin had been her reason for getting up every morning. It was impossible to stop wishing she were alive. Impossible for Nikki to stop thinking she'd sent her sister on that fateful trail ride.

And it was still hard to wrap her mind around Robert's pure evilness. At least he'd pay for his crimes. Hopefully prison wouldn't be kind to him. At some point, she knew she'd have to stop agonizing about the past. Just not yet.

Sonja's next client arrived so Nikki trudged back to her office, studiously averting her eyes from Gunner's empty dog bed. Maybe sitting in her car with a camera wouldn't be so bad. At least, it would get her out of the office. Still, it was impossible to rouse much enthusiasm about tracking down the tomcat that was stalking a neighbor's prized Pomeranian.

And that was the real source of her discontent. She'd become an investigator to help others avoid the pain her family had endured. Her mission to find Erin had buffered the fact that the majority of her cases were mind-numbing. She'd gladly search for missing children for free. But she needed the bread and butter clients to pay her bills.

Her phone buzzed. Justin's work number showed on the display and she jabbed the green button. Maybe he had a few extra minutes and they could meet for coffee.

"I'm waiting on warrants," Justin said. "Can you take a break? Want to come with me on a job?"

"Yes." She spoke so quickly that he chuckled, a low intimate sound that made her wish he was closer.

"Don't you want to know where we're going?"

"Doesn't matter. Anything beats tracking down an amorous stray cat."

"I'll pick you up in twenty minutes," he said. "Wear boots."

Eighteen minutes later she stood outside her office building, with hiking boots on her feet and several of Vinny's delicious Panini sandwiches bagged and gripped in her hand. She already knew Justin's eating times were scarce.

When she slid into his car, carrying the smell of deli and fresh toasted bread, Justin smiled in appreciation.

"Where are we going?" she asked, passing him a sandwich.

"Quarry Road." His eyes held hers as if studying her reaction. "I need to check the riding time from the barn to the clearing."

"Is that information for Savannah or Erin?"

He was already biting into his sandwich and she didn't repeat the question, respecting that there were aspects of his work he wouldn't share. Besides, she wanted to prove—even if it was just to herself—that her mind wasn't always wrapped around abductions. That she was able to share lighter moments and have fun. Normal people fun.

She nibbled on her lunch, automatically pulling off a piece of salami before remembering Gunner wasn't in the car.

"He'll be back with you soon," Justin said, "Tony says the water therapy will be a huge boost. And laser treatments have done wonders for dogs with similar injuries."

She nodded. Whatever Gunner needed, he'd have. No matter the cost. Even if it meant she'd have to work security at a shopping mall. "I better get a ramp built for when he comes home."

"I'll build it for you," Justin said. "And one at my house too...just in case."

His suggestive tone sent heat curling through her body. "In case I can't keep my hands off you?" she asked.

His laugh was quick and deep but he didn't voice the same sentiment, and that chipped away some of her glow. It wasn't as if she wanted to move in. Neither of them was ready for that. However, her confidence could do with a boost. Especially now that she didn't have Gunner or Robert or the hope of finding Erin. And she hated how she linked Robert in the same sentence with others so much more worthy.

She steered her thoughts to simpler topics and soon they slid into comfortable conversation: the best type of cheese in a Panini, noonday traffic patterns and whether the San Jose Sharks could ever lure an elite player like Nathan MacKinnon. In fact, they didn't talk shop at all and it was totally enjoyable, at least until Justin swung onto the rutted blacktop of Quarry Road.

She straightened, staring out the window, searching for the conspicuous white fences with a mix of eagerness and dread. When she was a kid, she'd looked forward to this drive. All her problems had faded away when she was around horses. Now the place just left tension knotting between her shoulder blades.

"What will happen to the stable?" she asked.

"The property is going up for sale. It may never open again, especially if a developer snaps it up."

She traced a finger over the side of the window. It was regrettable that the city was losing one of its few remaining spots to ride, but Savannah's tragedy left it unlikely any parent would want their child near the property, no matter if it had new owners. The stable simply had bad karma.

"My mom blamed horses for everything," Nikki said.

"So do you."

She turned her head, frowning. "No, I don't."

Justin just studied her, his expression surprisingly tender. He often looked unapproachable but right now his mouth was totally kissable. She already was familiar with the delightful ways he could use it on her body, and the knowledge created another wave of longing. That was certainly a better feeling than the tension that knotted her body the closer they drove to the stable. Erin had spent the last afternoon of her life here, and the barn wasn't a place Nikki wanted to linger.

"If we hurry," she said, "maybe we'll have time to stop at your house on the way back. Or mine, it's closer."

"Nothing I'd like more," he said, turning up the graveled driveway to the barn. "But we've got more important things to do today."

Nodding, she clenched her hands on her lap. Of course, she'd been joking although she wouldn't object to anything that would speed up this visit. Now that she knew the truth about Robert, it was impossible not to dissect all the times he had popped by the barn to watch them ride. Erin had never wanted Robert to take pictures of Nikki riding. She'd never wanted Nikki to sit in the front seat either. Nikki had never understood her sister's motives, had always thought Erin was being selfish.

And Nikki's single-minded focus on keeping their barn jobs had made it easier for Robert to corner Erin. Her mother had blamed the horses for her sister's disappearance, and she'd been right. But it had also been Nikki's fault.

"How long do you think *it* was going on?" she said, guessing Justin would know exactly what she was talking about.

Justin reached over, lacing his fingers through hers. "I don't know. And we never will. But I remember Robert bringing bananas, saying they were good nutrition. And you didn't like anything baked with bananas. At the time, I just thought he was playing favorites with his nieces." His voice thickened. "I should have guessed there was more to it."

She squeezed his hand. Obviously she wasn't the only one struggling with guilt. But there was no reason Justin should have noticed. Even her mother hadn't. And Robert had been clever, sliding in comments, driving wedges between them.

"I understand why Robert didn't want Mom and I being friends with a detective," she said. "But you never seemed to think much of Robert either. Why was that?"

Justin pulled to a stop behind the stable, reached forward and turned off the ignition.

"Why was that?" she repeated.

"He was a dirty cop," Justin said. "He sent you to Japan so you wouldn't hear the whispers. And he was always lying to your mother, making a big deal about how he shared her dislike for horses. The reality was he visited the track often. He was there the day you went with me but he ducked behind the crowd at the winner's circle so you wouldn't see him."

"But you never told me. Never said anything negative."

"You needed him," Justin said. "Your mother was sick and you had no one else but Robert."

I had you. But she sat silent and unmoving, only her mind spinning. Robert had always made sly innuendoes about Justin; she could see it now. But Justin hadn't retaliated. Not once. And he'd had so much more ammunition. Yet Justin had let her mother believe the worst of him.

He always did the right thing, never worrying what anyone thought. Even when he was a young man running the barn, he'd never bowed to the older, richer parents. He'd just done what was right—for the kids and the horses.

"You're much braver than me," she said.

Justin gave a disbelieving snort and jabbed his thumb toward the barn. "You're one of the most courageous people I know. Remember when that curly-haired guy tossed little Timmy in the manure pile, showing off for the older girls? You jumped right in, ready to fight the bullying, no matter the cost. You always stood up for the underdog. That helped me make the stable a better place. And this is the one spot you seemed truly happy."

She stared unseeingly out the window. Justin was trying to make her feel better, but the barn, the horses, the memories were all too entwined with losing Erin. The last time she'd been here she still had hope. Now though, it was obvious closure wasn't all that the therapists made it out to be. She felt hollow, along with the fear she'd carry this insidious grief for the rest of her life.

She fumbled for the door handle, suddenly needing fresh air.

"I hate like hell that your childhood was cut short," Justin said, reaching across her lap and lifting the handle. "Come on. Let's see what horses they have for us."

That got her attention. "Horses?" She twisted on the seat, the door half open. "What do you mean? You actually want to ride the trail?"

"That's right," he said, checking the lock on his metal gun box before unfolding from the car.

She pushed the door wider and stepped out, realizing now why he'd told her to wear boots. And riding was okay, she reassured herself, brushing away her dismay. It had been a long time since she'd been on a horse but if it involved gathering evidence for Erin or Savannah's cases, she wanted to help. Having a reason to be here made the visit easier.

A welcoming nicker grabbed her attention. Stormy was ambling across the sun-dried dirt of his paddock. The pony jammed his head over the middle rail, staring with hopeful eyes. For a timeless moment it felt as if she'd just stepped off the school bus.

Feeding him treats had been forbidden because of the pony's unfortunate tendency to nip. But she'd gathered carrots and apples from school lunch leftovers and brought them anyway, making sure Justin never noticed.

"That pony has a good memory," Justin said. "Appears he's still expecting treats."

Nikki laughed and gave his arm a little bump. "I thought you didn't know."

"Of course I knew. You were so happy when Stormy came to you like a dog, I didn't have the heart to stop it."

"That was nice of you," she said, bending and plucking some grass. "I hope he goes to a good home. He deserves a retirement place with lots of love."

"Unfortunately that's not how it works for horses like him," Justin said. "Parents buy safe ponies for their kids, not ones who buck and bite when they're not treated properly."

"But surely some child here wants him. You can't stop yourself from caring, even when the one you love is a challenge."

"True," he said. And the odd note in Justin's voice made her tilt her head, trying to read his expression.

"Detective Decker?" They wheeled toward the wiry man standing in the doorway of the barn.

"It's a good thing you came when you did," the man added, with a trace of impatience. "Your horses are saddled and waiting in the aisle. You'll have to grab a helmet and bridle them yourselves. I'm busy cataloguing for the auction."

He gestured with his clipboard and they left Stormy and followed him into the barn. Some of the stalls were already empty but two horses, a chestnut and a gray, were cross-tied in the aisle.

"Dobby and Duke," the man said, giving a chin jab. "They're being trailered to new owners tomorrow. Favorites like them sold quickly. By next week there won't be many horses left."

Nikki walked up to the chestnut gelding standing patiently in the aisle. Dobby had huge ears and a friendly eye, and was small enough that she could see over his back. She scratched his shoulder then his jaw, and he lowered his head, groaning in pleasure. It was obvious why he was a barn favorite. Everyone appreciated a horse that responded to attention.

"What happens to the ones that aren't sold?" she asked.

"They'll go through the auction." The man gave a pained shrug. "Who knows where they'll end up. Hopefully not Mexico." He was already turning away, his mind on other things. It wasn't just the horses who were losing their jobs but humans as well.

Nikki glanced at the empty stall that had housed Savannah's Arabian. The door was open, the floor swept clean of shavings. Someone had snapped her horse up quickly. At least Scooter didn't face an uncertain future. But the tragedy of it all left her thoughts heavy.

She adjusted Dobby's stirrups then slipped on the bridle, taking care not to bump his teeth with the snaffle bit, the movements coming naturally. She'd been so proud when Justin had let her tack up by herself, back when she'd first started working here. She felt him watching, ready to step in and help. But he just gave an approving nod and turned back to his own horse.

She followed Justin and Duke out of the barn, leading Dobby into the sunlight, hoping he didn't buck like Stormy. But he was far more patient than the pony had ever been, standing stock still while she checked the girth and mounted.

She peered toward the trees, at the trail Erin had followed on the last ride of her life, and then back at Justin. He still looked good on a horse, as relaxed and capable as when he'd leaped on Diesel and galloped into the woods. Searching for Erin. Finding only Pancho. And she realized this was probably just as hard on him.

"You obviously kept riding," she said, turning Dobby so she could avoid looking at the trail. "Did you continue as an instructor?"

"No. This stable was the end of my teaching days." His voice firmed. "Tighten your helmet."

She grinned, despite her melancholy. He may have thought he'd stopped teaching but he'd been the one who taught her how to drive a car, shoot a gun and handle a dog. He'd always stressed safety. And she could tell by the set of his jaw that they weren't riding out until her helmet was properly adjusted.

No doubt the police department was responsible for her safety, considering they were here to gather evidence. Justin knew she hadn't ridden in over a decade. If Dobby bucked, or even stumbled, there was a good chance she'd hit the ground. Naturally he was worried about liability.

"There," she said, after she adjusted her chinstrap. "You're always on top of the rules. I'm surprised you didn't make me sign a waiver."

He leaned over his horse's neck and rapped his knuckles on her helmet. Hard. It didn't hurt but it echoed uncomfortably in her ears. His reaction surprised her, especially since she'd meant the words as a compliment. "Is that a new way of checking tightness?" she asked.

"Just trying to knock some sense into your head," he said.

CHAPTER THIRTY-ONE

DOBBY HAD A SMOOTH and steady walk, and Nikki felt secure enough to turn in the saddle and watch the barn as it disappeared behind the trees. This was the same point on the trail where Erin had turned and waved. Happy, at least for the moment.

What had Erin been thinking? Had she been worrying about her math test or the guy in her chem lab or Robert? Or had she simply been enjoying the deep blue of the sky, the fresh pine smell and the luxury of escaping on a trail ride? Probably the latter, Nikki decided. It was impossible to stress about anything when riding. Something about a horse lulled the brain into a serene state. At least it did for her.

But Erin had obviously been upset when Pancho wouldn't jump the brook. She'd been angry and hurt when the boarders had deserted her, likely leading her to call Robert and ask him to pick her up by the bridge...resulting in a tragic chain of events.

Nikki's shoulders slumped and Dobby immediately slowed his steps. She gave his neck a pat, reassuring him that everything was okay.

"Stirrup length all right?" Justin asked, glancing over his shoulder.

"They're fine," she said. "Dobby is so used to looking after green riders, he thought I wanted to slow down."

"All good lesson horses are like that. But we can't go much slower. Ready to trot a bit?"

She nodded, noting a familiar oak tree. They'd always used the tree as a marker to show when their horses were warmed up. The trail was well groomed here with flat ground and no low branches. She squeezed Dobby into a trot, following Justin's lead and rising in the saddle, rather reassured she hadn't forgotten her old riding skills.

Minutes later they veered left, following the trail toward the clearing, their horses' hooves pounding a steady two-beat cadence. At this pace, with maybe a bit of a canter thrown in, they'd reach the clearing in another twenty minutes. It was odd to relive Erin's last ride, but it wasn't as disturbing as she'd anticipated.

In fact, a grin split her face when Justin nudged his horse into a canter and Dobby eagerly followed. It felt as if she'd been riding only yesterday, her seat secure and in sync with her horse, and she wondered why she'd given up something that was so much fun.

They reached a straight stretch where the branches formed a green canopy, shielding them from the overhead sun. She'd always loved this cooler section. She and Erin had often held their mounts back, waiting for Justin to round the corner so they had an excuse to gallop.

"Pretend Pancho and Stormy were upset at being alone," Erin had advised. "And that's why we had to go so fast. Just to catch up."

Justin glanced over his shoulder, checking on her and Dobby, and she caught the flash of his grin. Obviously he knew what she and Erin had done, what most every kid had done here, grabbing any excuse for more speed. But now he wasn't slowing his horse like a protective riding instructor. In fact, they were both galloping and it was every bit as exhilarating as it had been years ago.

Too soon, he slowed to a trot and it was a bit of shock to see they were approaching the clearing. It had always seemed further away. Even during the Savannah search, this area had felt remote. And gloomy. Now the sun broke through the leaves, dappling the ground and leaving it luminous.

Dobby arched his neck, tugging at the bridle, anticipating that they were going to jump the brook.

"Go for it," Justin called.

Nikki didn't stop to think. Her legs closed around Dobby and the horse surged across the clearing toward the brook. His head lowered, his muscles bunching, then they were soaring over the water and she couldn't hold back her delighted squeal. The brook wasn't nearly as wide as she remembered but it was definitely just as much fun. The best thing was she'd have to jump it again in order to rejoin Justin.

"Please don't critique my jumping position," she called. But her words came out in a bubble of laughter and she couldn't stop grinning.

She hadn't fallen off. Hadn't even worried about it, even though it had been more than a decade since she'd ridden. But her confidence was mostly because of Dobby. The lesson horses were always reliable, accustomed to jumping whether it was in the arena or on the trail. And she would definitely pick Dobby an apple, as a reward for his good behavior.

She trotted a circle, lining him up for the return jump. But thoughts of apples made her think of Erin, and she was midair above the brook when the realization hit. The lesson horses were safe and solid jumpers... Pancho had been a lesson horse.

She pulled Dobby to a stop as soon as they cleared the brook, her gaze clinging to Justin's face. "Pancho was a good jumper," she said.

Justin nodded.

"That means it was Erin who didn't want to jump the brook," Nikki said. "She was the one who wanted to dismount. To leave the other girls."

"Yes." He gave another nod.

"But that means she chose to see Robert." Nikki's voice trailed off, chewing over the fact. She'd blamed herself for enabling Erin to go on that trail ride, a ride that had resulted in her sister running to Robert for solace. But he lived twenty miles away; his office had been even further.

"She must have called him," Nikki said slowly. "It was all planned. That's why she wanted to go for a ride. So she could meet him privately." Nikki gripped the reins a little tighter. "The whole time I was blaming the boarders when it wasn't their fault."

"No," Justin said. "It wasn't."

He didn't repeat what he'd been saying for the past twelve years but the unspoken message hung in the air. *It hadn't been Nikki's fault either.* And the knowledge burned her eyes while at the same time a great weight lifted from her shoulders.

"I'm going to get Dobby an apple," she said. "And take one back to Stormy too. Is it okay? Do we have time?" The words bubbled out, so light and airy it was surprising Justin even understood them. She was grinning too much and seconds later she was crying and she had no idea why.

But Justin understood. He dismounted and, in one fluid motion, scooped her from the saddle. "Let it go, sweetheart," he whispered, holding both horses' reins and tucking her into his chest. "You found her. It's over."

"No wonder the detectives always thought it was a boyfriend," she said, hiccupping into his shirt. "But I was too stubborn. Blaming it on horses. Men. Me."

And maybe Erin had been trying to tell her something, through Sonja, when she'd told Nikki to pick apples. To be happy. Horses had always made her happy.

She lifted her head, not caring about the tears streaming down her cheeks. "I'm going to start riding again. And I'm going to buy Stormy. He deserves a good retirement. That will make Gunner happy too and it will be like having part of Erin close. We had so much fun here, with the kids, with the horses, with you."

Justin's eyes darkened. "You always had me."

She shrugged. This wasn't the best time to bring up his string of girlfriends. Or that his first love was his job. She'd be rushing out the door too, gone for days, if she had cases that actually mattered.

"So, what do you think?" she asked. "Should I buy Stormy?"

"Now that you're financially independent," Justin said, "you can buy any horse you want."

"What do you mean?"

"Didn't the benefits people call you? My lawyer confirmed it. Since your dad's death wasn't a suicide, his insurance will kick in along with a lump sum death payment and a big bump in pension, all retroactive. I think we can push that too, since it was at the hands of another cop."

She gripped his arms, stunned to silence. It seemed there was no need to worry about Gunner's vet bill after all. The knowledge was bittersweet considering how much her Mom had struggled. Sometimes people needed a little help. Unfortunately her mother had turned to the wrong person.

Justin lifted his arm and thumbed the tears from her cheek. But he didn't speak, ever patient. One of the horses grabbed a bite of grass and the sound of chewing was loud in the serene clearing.

"I want to help people," she said slowly. "People who have no one else. Like you did for me."

"You'll be good at it. And now you can focus on the cases you want. Just promise me you'll be careful, and stay safe."

They both knew that was a promise she couldn't make although she certainly felt safe now, along with another sensation, the melting want she always felt whenever Justin touched her.

But his words sounded suspiciously like a kiss-off. After all, they'd found Erin. The burden of guilt they'd carried was gone. Along with their special tie.

"Is that why you gave me Gunner? So you wouldn't have to look after me?" She hid her dismay behind a breezy smile but her chest felt as if it was shrinking. Life without Justin would be unimaginable. And if he returned to his parade of women, it would be devastating.

She hadn't regretted sleeping with him. Until now. But she didn't want to be an anchor around his neck either, binding him to her because she had no one else.

"I get it," she said, her face still locked in a twisted smile. "It was a bad time and you felt obliged to help. Now that it's over, I totally understand why you're moving on."

His eyes widened. A sound escaped, a noise halfway between a grunt and a choke. Then he pulled her into his chest and she could feel the shaking of his shoulders.

"I'm never leaving," he said, his mouth curved against her cheek. "You must know that by now. For me, there is no moving on. Ever."

He said something else, something muffled, his voice no longer amused, only tender. But she didn't need more words. Because he was holding her like he never intended to let go. And then his lips found hers in an embrace that was much more than a kiss.

It felt like a promise.

OTHER BOOKS BY BEV PETTERSEN

About the Author

BEV PETTERSEN IS A three-time nominee in the National Readers Choice Award and a two-time finalist in the Romance Writers of America's Golden Heart® Contest as well as the winner of other international awards including the Reader Views Reviewer's Choice Award, Aspen Gold Reader's Choice Award, NEC-RWA Reader's Choice Award, Write Touch Readers' Award, a Kirkus Recommended Read, and a HOLT Medallion Award of Merit. She competed for five years on the Alberta Thoroughbred race circuit and is an Equestrian Canada certified coach.

Bev lives in Nova Scotia with her family—humans and four-legged—and when she's not writing novels, she's riding. If you'd like to know about special offers or when her next book will be available, please visit her at http://www.BevPettersen.com where you can sign up for a newsletter.

Made in the USA
Las Vegas, NV
23 January 2023